# ROBIN HOOD

## [D]RONES, DAMS & DESTRUCTION

# ROBERT MUCHAMORE'S
# ROBIN HOOD

## DRONES, DAMS & DESTRUCTION

HOT
KEY
BOOKS

First published in Great Britain in 2022 by
HOT KEY BOOKS
4th Floor, Victoria House, Bloomsbury Square
London WC1B 4DA
Owned by Bonnier Books
Sveavägen 56, Stockholm, Sweden
www.hotkeybooks.com

A CIP catalogue record for this book is available from the British Library.

ISBN: 978-1-4714-0951-6
*Also available as an ebook and in audio*

1

Typeset by DataConnection Ltd
Printed and bound in Great Britain by Clays Ltd, Elcograf S.p.A.

Hot Key Books is an imprint of Bonnier Books UK
www.bonnierbooks.co.uk

# ROBIN HOOD

# THE STORY SO FAR . . .

**Things are bad in Sherwood Forest . . .**

Evil gangster **Guy Gisborne** has the declining industrial town of Locksley under his thumb, controlling everything from petty drug deals to senior judges.

He works in an uneasy alliance with the Sheriff of Nottingham, **Marjorie Kovacevic**.

The ambitious Sheriff likes to portray herself as a successful businesswoman and get-tough politician who locks up criminals and cracks down on immigration. But deep in the forest, Sheriff Marjorie's army of private guards deals brutally with anyone who gets in her way.

**But the people are fighting back!**

When **Ardagh Hood** dared to speak out about corruption in Locksley, Guy Gisborne had him beaten, framed and sent to jail.

His thirteen-year-old son **Robin Hood** escaped to the forest, joined a band of rebels based in an abandoned outlet mall and mounted a series of daring raids and heroic rescues.

For his many fans, Robin is a hero leading the fight against injustice. But cops and the government say Robin and his rebel friends are terrorists who must be hunted down and thrown in jail.

# 1. YOU STEPPED IN SOMETHING

Record-breaking summer rain had flooded vast tracts of Sherwood Forest, and for the first time in decades the Macondo River ran deep enough to take a boat the three hundred kilometres from Lake Victoria to the Eastern Delta.

The rains had continued into October and Robin Hood was sick of it, from emptying drip buckets in the night to stop his den flooding, to the mushroom stench of mould and clinging humidity that made him sweat through clean clothes in the time it took to tie his boots.

Robin sat in an open-hulled boat, trying to read a book with damp crinkled pages, while rain pelted a thick tarp that covered him up to the neck. Lanky trees blocked most of the daylight, as an outboard motor moved the boat at a crawl.

Lyla Masri had been charged with keeping Robin and his best friend Marion Maid out of mischief. She sat on a plank at the boat's rear, steering. She had a

Russian assault rifle propped between muddy legs and kept a careful eye on the deck compass. It was easy to lose the river's path on the flooded plains and this was one of many spots where satnav signals didn't reach the forest floor.

Robin's head felt fuzzy. His brain refused entry to the words on the page and he'd read the same line four times when Marion's boot nudged his ankle. She sat across from Robin, sharing the big tarp, her head protected with a wide-brimmed rain hat whose goofy neon strap looped around her chin.

'That your Chemistry homework?' Marion asked.

Robin thought about holding the book up so Marion could see the cover, but moving risked draining puddled water from the tarp into his lap.

'I downloaded crib notes,' Marion continued. 'You can copy my answers if you like.'

Robin sounded grumpy. 'It's not homework. It's a book about the Magic Cheese.'

Marion looked baffled. 'Magic *what*?'

'Magic Cheese were legendary computer hackers back in olden times. They did wild stuff. Developed the first computer virus, built the first scorpions to track mobile phone signals. They almost wound up in jail, but the CIA recruited them to hack the Chinese.'

Marion wasn't a big reader and looked unimpressed. 'I don't know how you get through. What is that, five hundred pages?'

Robin slapped the book shut. Marion wasn't the reason he'd read the same paragraph six times, but he blamed her anyway. 'How can I read if you keep interrupting?'

'My first words in half an hour,' Marion growled back.

As Robin rolled his eyes, Marion pulled a pack of chocolate-covered peanuts from her backpack. She tipped a dozen into her palm and put on a show, dropping them into her mouth one at a time as Robin pretended he wasn't interested.

'Want some, grumpy guts?' Marion asked. She rattled the bag.

As Robin leaned forward, Lyla steered the open-hulled boat between an embankment and a huge lightning-charred trunk.

'Ta,' Robin said.

But as he tried to take the chocolates Marion flicked her boot up, spraying him with rainwater pooled on the tarp.

'What was that for?' Robin gasped, as it went in his eyes and trickled inside his hoodie.

As Marion cracked up laughing, Robin flicked wet hair out of his eyes. He realised Marion had put serious thought into the prank because she had her phone filming it.

'Turn it off!' Robin said, as he made a grab.

'Got you in glorious slow motion,' Marion said. 'Your expression was gold!'

As Robin tried to get Marion's phone, she burrowed under the tarp and started crawling down the wooden hull towards the rear. But Robin managed to dig fingers down her trailing boot and yank her back.

The boat was too large for the wrestling to make it unstable, and Lyla smirked as she watched them tussle under the tarp.

'Delete or I'll dunk your head!' Robin yelled.

But Marion got free by yanking her foot out of the boot.

'It's going online,' Marion yelled as she crawled down the boat. 'I'll call it *Butt Face Gets a Soaking.*'

'What did you step in?' Robin said, making a gagging sound. 'This boot reeks!'

Lyla watched Robin reach out of the tarp and try to dangle Marion's boot over the water. But Marion straddled his chest and snatched it back.

'Get your bum off my face!' Robin demanded.

'Fart's a-coming!' Marion said. 'Inhale my breakfast, loser.'

As Robin escaped and clattered into a stack of empty cargo boxes, Lyla decided they were getting too crazy. 'Enough!' she roared as she grabbed the tangled tarp and stripped it away.

The two thirteen-year-olds were sprawled over empty boxes, breathless, soggy and smirking.

'We're still a couple of hours from Locksley,' Lyla continued. 'I'd better not hear either of you moan that you're cold or thirsty, or . . .'

Lyla stopped abruptly because she was only twenty and realised she sounded like her mother.

The teenagers straightened their clothes and stacked the boxes they'd knocked over. Robin reached for a plastic tub and used it to bail rainwater over the side, while Marion realised she really had stepped in something nasty and leaned over the side, washing the sole of her boot in the spray coming off the bow.

'I need a snack and my shirt is itchy,' Robin said, putting on a baby voice to wind Lyla up.

At the bow, Marion shot upright. Her dripping boot twirled by its laces and she looked alarmed.

'Did you hear?' she blurted.

'What?' Robin asked as he shook drips off his Magic Cheese book.

'Gunshot,' Marion said.

Lyla looked doubtful, but she couldn't hear much of anything sat near the outboard motor.

'Sherwood's full of weird noises,' Robin said dismissively.

They couldn't risk ploughing into bandits, so Lyla cut the motor. The forest soundscape of birds, bugs and lapping water went uninterrupted long enough for Marion to feel stupid, but as Lyla reached around to restart the engine there was a squeal from a tiny human.

'Mummy, she's hurting me.'

Something muffled the little voice, making Robin queasy at the thought of a little kid getting hurt. The echo in the canopy made the sound hard to pinpoint, but it wasn't far away.

# 2. LET'S DO A HATE CRIME

The speedy, aluminium-hulled launch was brand-new, without a scuff or dent. Kenny, a ball of tattoos and body hair, stood at the wheel wearing camouflage and wraparound sunglasses. His companion, Shannon, was propped on her elbows on the raised foredeck. She surveyed the flooded plain through binoculars and her head was topped with a **SHERIFF MARJORIE FOR PRESIDENT** baseball cap.

'Refugee scum by the embankment,' Shannon said eagerly as she pointed left.

The bow dipped as Kenny cut the engine. He glanced at the navigation console. Its useless screen flashing **NO SIGNAL** in big red letters.

'Look dangerous?' Kenny asked warily.

Shannon was the more confident of the pair. She vaulted the sleek boat's windshield and slapped Kenny on the back as her boots clomped down in the cockpit.

'See for yourself, Captain.'

Kenny took the binoculars and smiled. A couple of hundred metres away an exhausted man pushed a raft through shallow water, close to a steep embankment ridged with massive tree roots. The raft's buoyancy came from plastic water dispenser bottles lashed together with nylon rope, while the deck was a rotten door.

'I made sturdier rafts at Boy Scouts,' Kenny scoffed, as he realised a couple of scruffy kids sat on the raft. The scabby-kneed toddler was probably a boy, his head resting in the lap of a girl no older than ten. Stacked around them were cooking pots, a rolled-up tent and knotted plastic rubbish sacks.

'Idiots should have left the flood zone months ago,' Shannon said.

'Shall we have fun?' Kenny asked.

Shannon showed off nice teeth as she smiled. 'Refugees crawling out of Sherwood like worms, taking our country over. Let's show 'em who's boss!'

'Damn right!' Kenny said, opening the throttle. 'Get your gun in case they bite back.'

The nippy little boat made a tight turn as it accelerated. In less than twenty seconds it swooped around a muddy embankment, frightened a hundred wading birds into the air and charged at the crudely built raft.

As they closed in, Kenny saw that the family was completed by a woman. She squelched close to the embankment, holding a rope so the raft didn't get dragged into the current.

'Slow down, slow down!' the man pushing the raft shouted frantically, as his daughter leaped up waving a coloured towel like a flag.

Kenny put on full throttle as Shannon took out her phone to film.

'Refugee scum!' Shannon announced for the benefit of future viewers. 'Defend our culture! Marjorie for President!'

The woman at the side of the raft realised what was about to happen, screaming, 'Jump!' to her daughter as she grabbed her toddler son.

The wash from the launch threw the raft sideways. At the closest point, Kenny flicked the boat away from shore so the raft got the full blast from his propellers.

'Yippie-kay-aye!' Shannon whooped, punching the air as her phone filmed the pitiful family clambering onto the muddy embankment while everything they owned tipped into the water.

'Get welfare in your own country!' Kenny added, as he took his hand off the throttle.

Once they were sure their two children were planted on the embankment, the desperate parents waded back to the raft. The brightly coloured ropes that held it together had slipped loose and all their stuff was in the water.

'They look Indian,' Shannon said.

Kenny shrugged. 'Shall I do another blast past? Splinter what's left!'

'It's Indian tradition,' Shannon said thoughtfully.

'What are you talking about?' Kenny asked.

'Indian brides get gold when they marry. And they carry gold because the money in their country is worthless.'

'You think those soggy dirtbags have gold?' Kenny sneered.

'Let's find out,' Shannon said determinedly. 'What's the worst that could happen?'

As the launch turned back towards the family, the mother and father gave up on wading out to rescue their possessions and tried getting further up the muddy embankment. But they only made it a few steps before Shannon skimmed a bullet over the mother's head.

'Give us your gold, money, smartphones,' she said as she leaped off the side of the moving boat.

The embankment mud was so thick, Shannon lost her footing. The father took a half-step forward, his terrified son gripping his right leg.

'I have seventy pounds,' he said, trembling.

As Kenny tied the launch to a sturdy branch, he couldn't help noticing that, while the family had dark skin, their accents were local. But Shannon was determined to prove her theory about Indian gold, so she jammed her rifle in the dad's chest, then grabbed the small boy hiding behind him.

'What's your name, brat?' she asked, dragging the toddler through a puddle as he exploded in tears.

The boy didn't answer. But he squealed when Shannon squeezed his tiny hand.

'Mummy, she's hurting me,' the boy screamed.

'Please,' his mother begged tearfully. 'Look at us! Look at our clothes. My phone is held together with tape, my daughter's boots are too small. You think we'd be pushing a raft upriver if we had any other choice?'

Kenny realised that people this desperate didn't have hidden caches of gold and his expression was rueful as he looked at Shannon.

'We're wasting our time, let's get out of here.'

'Foreigners lie,' Shannon snarled as she flung the toddler sideways into the mud. 'Show me gold or I'll drown this brat under my boot.'

'I was born in Locksley,' the father shouted back furiously. 'I drove a taxi. We ran to the forest after Gisborne's thugs forced me to deliver drugs and said they'd kill my family if I got caught.'

'Let our son go,' the mother pleaded.

Before Shannon could consider the demand there was a thwack, followed by a fleshy squelch. The toddler crawled over mud to his dad as Shannon crashed down, screaming in pain with an arrow speared through her thigh.

Kenny looked shocked and tried scrambling back to the boat. But Robin Hood stood at the top of the steep embankment with an arrow aimed right at him.

# 3. HOW TO DEAL WITH DIRTBAGS

'What kind of dirtbag?' Lyla demanded, as she gave Shannon the hardest kick she'd ever given anyone. 'Who tortures a three-year-old?'

Lyla was angry enough to dish out more punishment, but other things had to be considered. *Who were the bad guys? Did they have friends nearby? And what to do with a desperate family who'd lost everything they owned?*

Glancing back over her shoulder, Lyla was glad to see the kids being practical. Marion was using their boat to retrieve belongings floating downriver, while Robin put on a tough-guy act, forcing Kenny to kneel in the mud then using rope from the disintegrated raft to hog-tie his wrists to his ankles.

'You saved us,' the tearful dad kept repeating, clutching his hands over his heart as his wife and kids held him. 'We had nothing to give them.'

Once Kenny's feet were tied, Robin checked him over and noticed that he had all the best gear. A carbon-fibre hunting knife, fancy boots, designer sunglasses and night-vision goggles. And all pristine, like he'd never been in the forest before.

After swiping the goggles and sliding on Kenny's fancy sunglasses, Robin extracted a bulging wallet from his tactical vest. Kenny must have cleaned out his wallet once a decade, but among wodges of restaurant bills, discount cards, parking vouchers and dry-cleaning stubs, Robin found a newly minted Sherwood Castle employee card.

'Kenny Eggard,' Robin read aloud. 'Sherwood Castle Security Officer, date of employment 9th October. That's three whole days ago.'

'One of Sheriff Marjorie's new recruits,' Lyla said, giving the tied man a nasty grin. 'Getting much job satisfaction so far, Kenny?'

Kenny flinched, fearing a kick like the one Lyla had given Shannon. But that was a special service for people who tortured toddlers and Lyla just flicked her toe, splashing muddy water in his face.

'I'll check out the boat,' Robin said.

As Robin climbed aboard he saw Marion fifty metres downriver, using a bargepole to retrieve a bag of clothes snagged on overhanging branches.

'Boat's as fresh as their equipment,' Robin yelled to Lyla as he saw **NO SIGNAL** blinking on the navigation screen. 'But they're a long way from Sherwood Castle and I'll bet they got lost.'

'That means they don't have friends nearby,' Lyla answered thoughtfully, as Shannon let out a low moan and the dripping ten-year-old girl waded up to Robin on the boat.

'I know you're Robin Hood!' she said brightly.

Robin nodded. 'Bow and arrow is a giveaway,' he joked.

'Daddy.' The girl beamed, looking behind. 'Can you *believe* we got rescued by Robin Hood?'

As Robin inspected the boat his newest fan kept nattering. 'I wanted a bow and arrow for my birthday. But Daddy does driving jobs and there's been no work lately. So my birthday presents were only clothes. But my new clothes were hanging up to dry when the mudslide knocked down our hut. We lost all our drinking water and the nice neighbours up the hill drowned in the mudslide. So we had to leave.'

The little Castle Guard launch had a small area behind the wheel with a couple of bench seats and a raised foredeck. As Robin listened to his chatty fangirl, he realised there was a storage area in the bow.

'Bingo!' Robin announced, as he spotted the latch for a sliding panel next to the steering column.

The light came on automatically, and since the boat was new, Robin hoped he'd find some useful equipment. But what he saw made him gasp.

'Sooo nasty . . .' Robin purred, as he dived into the crawl space.

Lyla looked around as Robin backed out of the storage bay holding up a taco-shaped bear trap. The spring-loaded trap had vicious metal spikes, and while the name came from the trap's ability to catch bears, they were just as painful and deadly to humans who stepped in one.

Lyla fought the urge to deliver another kick.

'Maybe a hundred traps in here,' Robin said.

Lyla bent over Kenny. 'Are you proud, big guy?' she spat. 'Spend your days setting traps that'll tear a person's foot off. When that gets boring, you torment a desperate family for kicks.'

Marion was pulling up in the wooden boat. 'I got six black bags and most of the cookware,' she yelled, slightly out of breath. 'Clothes mostly stayed dry in the bags, but plates and crockery are all smashed.'

'Check this out,' Robin said, showing Marion the trap.

Marion scowled as her boots splattered on the muddy embankment and she tied off their boat.

'I heard Castle Guards had been spreading traps through the forest,' Marion said. 'There's been loads of injuries in Dr Gladys's clinic.'

'We think these scumbags were out here alone,' Lyla told Marion. 'But I'd rather not stick around longer than we have to.'

Marion got her first proper look at the family they'd rescued. She didn't know their names, but she'd seen them at the weekly market at Designer Outlets, with the dad buying meat and bread while the mum queued to get the kids a hot shower.

'Where were you trying to get to with that raft?' Lyla asked the mother.

But the dad answered. 'If we'd known the floods would get this bad we'd have left the area. The last surge downriver set off a huge mudslide, leaving our shelter engulfed.'

'We lost our drinking water,' the mother added, embarrassed. 'Our only option was to lash that pathetic raft together and try to reach Will Scarlock's people at Designer Outlets.'

'I'm on the security team at Designer Outlets,' Lyla explained, as she pointed to the Castle Guard boat. 'It's an hour's cruise if you take that.'

The father nodded, but still looked wary. 'We heard that Designer Outlets is swamped with flood victims and they're not taking more people in.'

Lyla shook her head. 'The non-stop rain has damaged the mall roof. We're short of everything and a lot of flood victims are camping in the parking lots. We're encouraging everyone who can to move onto higher ground in the west. But we'd never turn away someone in need.'

Seeing their raft destroyed and the toddler tortured had left the family numb. Marion had saved most of their stuff and they had a good boat instead of the raft. But they were too exhausted to show relief as Robin helped load the salvaged possessions into the Castle Guard vessel.

While Marion used her boating experience to make sure they had enough fuel and programmed the mall's location into the navigation unit, Lyla handed the mother Shannon's rifle and showed her how to use it.

'Head towards the sun,' Marion said. 'Once you're a couple of kilometres north-west of here the trees thin out and you'll pick up satellite navigation.'

'You can't come with us?' the father asked.

'We're heading the other way,' Lyla explained. 'These teenage horrors have business in Locksley. I'll buy a boatload of supplies and we'll head back to Designer Outlets in the morning.'

'When you get to the mall, tell security about those bear traps,' Marion added.

'We've got welding gear,' Lyla said, nodding in agreement. 'We'll slice them up so they don't fall back into the wrong hands.'

'Absolutely,' the mother agreed.

'You're my hero, Robin Hood!' the daughter yelled, giving a wave as the boat pulled away.

Marion tutted and scowled at Robin. 'Yeah, because you did *everything*.'

Robin laughed. 'Marion, you've got to face up to the fact that I'm adorable.'

Marion grunted. 'Those wraparound sunglasses make you look like a total knob.'

'Stop mucking around, this is dangerous territory,' Lyla reminded them, then turned to look at the two rookie

Castle Guards. 'But what to do with these fine specimens of humanity?'

Kenny was hog-tied and shivering as his bulk gradually sank into the slushy mud. Shannon's moans were getting weaker, because she had an arrow stuck through her leg and was close to losing consciousness.

'I'd happily put a bullet through their nasty skulls,' Lyla said, loud enough for both captives to hear. 'But Will Scarlock says we have to respect everyone's human rights.'

'But we can't hold prisoners in an open boat,' Marion said.

'And leaving 'em here is as bad as killing them,' Robin added.

Lyla squatted in the mud between the two captives and tried to think of a solution as fresh rain pelted the ground. Seeing Shannon's **SHERIFF MARJORIE FOR PRESIDENT** cap sticking out of the mud gave her inspiration.

'Once we're a few kilometres clear, I'll call Sherwood Castle and let them know your position,' Lyla told them. 'Sheriff Marjorie can decide whether it's worth sending someone down here to save your sorry asses.'

# 4. MACONDO MADNESS FUN PARK

While Sheriff Marjorie was an ambitious politician, expanding her private army of Castle Guards and doing all she could to make life tough for Forest People, Guy Gisborne only cared about making money.

With floods blocking most land routes between the town of Locksley and Sherwood Forest, the Macondo River had become a choke point, but Gisborne let Forest People trade, if their boats paid mooring fees to his goons and bought overpriced supplies from his warehouses.

But Gisborne would never forgive Robin for shooting him in the balls, and the teenager's heart thudded as he peeked over the side of the boat into the heart of the gangster's territory.

The Macondo was a hundred metres wide by the time it reached Locksley. Lyla cut the engine and drifted towards the north riverbank and the sunset silhouette of Velociraptor, a decaying quad loop rollercoaster that had once been the star attraction of Macondo Madness Fun Park.

'My aunt texted to say she's waiting in the parking lot,' Marion said, as the boat thumped against the tyres hung over the side of a tatty pontoon dock. 'Says there's no sign of Gisborne's people.'

'Keep your eyes peeled anyway,' Lyla warned, as Robin hopped ashore and Marion threw out their bows and backpacks. 'Follow the path beneath the rollercoaster – there's a gap in the fence by the turnstiles.'

Robin ran with his bow in hand in case there was trouble, but was more wary of getting crapped on by flocks of birds perched in the rollercoaster as he followed Marion along an overgrown footpath.

'Ever ride Velociraptor?' she asked.

'This place closed when I was a baby.'

They heard Lyla powering away in the boat as Marion ducked through the holed fence. Her Aunt Lucy stood outside by a battered white hatchback.

'Getting taller,' Lucy told her niece as she pulled her into a hug.

Robin wasn't sure he was hug-worthy, but Lucy grabbed him tight and kissed his cheek. 'You are rock solid!' Lucy said. 'Have you been working out?'

Robin *loved* being complimented on his physique, but was less happy when Lucy looked down her nose and said, 'Nice sunglasses', in a tone that suggested the opposite.

'Seatbelts,' Lucy reminded the pair as they set off across the abandoned theme park's empty parking lot, then up a concrete ramp that merged with a deserted six-lane highway. 'Marion has time to eat and scrub up at my flat before we head to the hospital. So we'll drop Robin off first.'

'Do you know where you're taking me?' Robin asked.

'It's a new building by the university,' Lucy said, as the car turned onto a rusting truss bridge over the Macondo River. 'Student housing.'

'Near where I grew up?' Robin asked.

Lucy nodded. 'They've started building one of Gisborne's landfill dumps out that way,' she warned. 'They're knocking houses down.'

Marion grew up in the forest, so even a dilapidated city like Locksley was a novelty. She gawped out of the window, enjoying sunset on the river and the long shadows cast by buildings in the centre of town.

There was zero traffic as they cruised a deserted residential area west of the city centre. Rows of low-rise blocks which once housed factory workers had been abandoned for decades and were gradually being reclaimed by nature.

As Lucy had warned, Robin's old neighbourhood was being cleared and turned into a garbage dump. Side streets Robin had run or biked hundreds of times had been fenced off and had signs with the green tree logo of Gisborne Environmental Waste Management.

'Gisborne's a git,' Marion said when she saw Robin's sad expression. 'Runs Locksley into the ground, then makes millions using the land to bury everyone else's trash.'

'Not far now,' Lucy warned Robin. 'Send a message so they can let you straight inside.'

Minutes later the hatchback stopped by an eight-storey student accommodation block. A woman in a wheelchair opened a green fire-exit door from inside.

'See you guys tomorrow,' Robin said as he reached into the back seat for his stuff.

'Enjoy your meal,' Lucy said.

'Try not to do anything dumb for once,' Marion added.

'Hope you get on OK at the hospital,' Robin told Marion as he kicked the car door shut and jogged across a stretch of pavement.

Robin felt tearful as he hugged the woman in the wheelchair. 'Auntie Pauline.' Robin sniffed. 'I've *really* missed you.'

'Missed you too, buster,' Pauline said, as she rolled back inside. 'Let's get you upstairs and out of sight.'

# 5. ROASTIES AND REUNIONS

Pauline Hood wheeled across a smart lobby, with manufacturer's stickers still on the glass in the revolving door and artificial plants clad in bubble wrap.

'Nice digs,' Robin said, as he glanced about.

Pauline nodded as she hit the up button for the elevators. 'Brand-new,' she said proudly. 'Two hundred and eighty rooms. Students move in next week, and they'll break *everything* by Christmas.'

Robin laughed as a lift arrived. For as long as he could remember, his aunt had been Chief Housing Officer for the university. Cheap land and housing meant the university prospered as the rest of the town declined, and Pauline's job was to find decent places for thousands of students to live.

'The number-one question from every student used to be *Will I have to share a bathroom?*' Pauline told her nephew as they rode to the top floor. 'Now they see my name and ask *Are you related to Robin Hood?*'

Robin laughed. 'Sorry, Auntie!'

'I'm proud of what you've done,' Pauline said. 'But I've grown grey hairs worrying about you.'

'Have Gisborne's people hassled you?'

'Nothing I can't handle,' Pauline answered. 'You get thick-skinned when you live on wheels.'

'But we're not meeting at your house,' Robin noted.

'Better safe than sorry.'

The lift opened into a wide eighth-floor hallway, with bay windows at each end and rows of walnut doors with hotel-style card locks. Robin smelled fresh paint and good food as he glanced about.

'It's not all this posh,' Pauline explained. 'Top two floors are for wealthy overseas students, who subsidise rent for the ordinary kids down below.'

Robin looked unconvinced. 'Why would rich students come to this dump?'

'They think Locksley's hip, believe it or not,' Pauline said, as they approached an apartment with the door propped open and lights on inside. 'Hipster kids who've been to fancy boarding schools, studying art in Locksley, playing pool in dive bars and attending raves in abandoned warehouses.'

Robin's stomach growled as he got closer to the apartment. His dad was a terrible cook and his favourite childhood meal had been Auntie's Sunday roast.

'Can I smell beef?'

'Slow-cooked brisket with red wine and shallots,' Pauline agreed. 'And your favourite dessert.'

'Pear and custard tart?' Robin said cheerfully.

'I made extra pie for you to take back to Designer Outlets and share with the people who've been looking after you.'

Robin followed his aunt into an open-plan apartment, which had high ceilings, a pool table in the lounge and a gigantic teenager peering into the hot oven.

'Baste it, don't taste it,' Pauline ordered, then picked a spatula off the kitchen island and used it to fondly whack Little John on the bum.

'I'm not eating,' Robin's half-brother said.

But a sizzling-hot roast potato bulged his cheek as he shut the oven door.

'Wassup, bruv!' Robin said, sweeping past his aunt's chair and reaching up to give his gigantic brother a slap on the shoulder. 'Happy birthday.'

'Good to see you, titch,' John said cheerfully.

'Seventeen!' Pauline said. 'I swear it was yesterday you were in my lap sucking a dummy.'

'You've got stubble!' Robin told Little John. 'And I didn't get you a birthday present, since your ma is Sheriff Marjorie and she probably got you a Ferrari and a villa on Skegness Island.'

'She's not *that* rich,' Little John said, buying into the joke. 'It was only a BMW and a condo.'

As Robin looked at the amazing pear tarts and beef joint in the oven, Pauline handed Robin two shopping bags filled with clothes.

24

'I asked some students what brands boys are wearing,' Pauline explained. 'So hopefully my picks aren't too tragic.'

'I might shower and put this on before we eat,' Robin said, as he held up a plaid shirt to check the size.

John and Pauline looked shocked. Robin had been the kind of kid who'd fester in the same outfit for a week and only bathe if he got thrown in the tub. But after six months in the forest, the appeal of hot showers and fluffy towels had grown.

As Robin tugged his hoodie over his head, Little John checked the time on his phone and looked at Pauline.

'We've only got two minutes,' John said. 'Piglet will have to shower after.'

'Two minutes until what?' Robin asked, as he realised his filthy hoodie had showered the floor with flakes of dry mud.

Pauline and John smirked and exchanged a knowing look.

'Tell me,' Robin said, desperate to know the big secret. 'Are you two playing a joke on me?'

'Yeah.' John laughed. 'My mum's gonna jump out of a big cake and adopt you.'

'I need to pee,' Robin said. 'Is there time for that?'

The apartment's main bathroom had a fancy shower with six heads pointing in different directions and a toilet seat that rose automatically when Robin got close. When he came out, flicking water off his hands because there was no towel, Little John and Pauline had moved to a laptop on the kitchen island.

'He was waiting for us to log in,' Little John told Robin excitedly. 'They do electronic sweeps, so he can't stay online for long.'

'We've both been able to visit,' Pauline said. 'So you can do the talking.'

Robin jogged across the floor and saw a blurry video call on the laptop. The man on screen had a long beard and squatted in a cramped spot between a metal toilet and the end of a narrow bunk.

'Dad!' Robin choked, as his eyes filled with tears. 'How'd you get a phone in your cell?'

# 6. MARION AND THE HOT MEDIC

After a wash, change and fishfinger sandwich at Aunt Lucy's apartment, Marion jumped back in the little hatchback and set off for Locksley General.

The sprawling Gothic pile was the first hospital built in Locksley and the last to stay open as the town's population collapsed. Many windows in the facade were cracked or boarded, while the stonework was tar black from decades of industrial pollution.

The only modern bit of Locksley General was a bunker-like lobby extension with barred windows, airport-style security and a checkpoint staffed by armed cops.

Patients and visitors needed a National Identity Card to enter the hospital. Since Marion lived in an illegal forest dwelling and went to an unregistered school, she didn't have one and would be arrested and thrown into juvenile detention if she rocked up at the checkpoint.

Fortunately, many hospital staff either sympathised with Forest People or were happy to make extra cash doing off-the-books treatments.

'You'll go in through the loading dock,' Lucy said, as she pulled up in a busy visitors' lot and opened an app to pay for parking.

'Have you done this before?' Marion asked, studying the loading bay's battered metal shutters.

Lucy nodded. 'There's always someone in the forest who needs treatment. I've been up here three times since the government's big clampdown on fake identity cards.'

This reminder made Marion nervous. Her sixteen-year-old cousin, Freya Tuck, had broken her leg on a mission to infiltrate Sherwood Castle a few months earlier. The rebels had taken Freya to a hospital north of Sherwood Forest. She got admitted for emergency treatment with a fake identity card, but was arrested when she tried to leave. Now she was in prison, awaiting trial for rebel activities that the government called terrorism.

'Chuma is a top guy,' Lucy told her niece, then scowled at the parking app. 'They've put parking up to six pounds an hour. It's robbery!'

Marion bounced her trainers and bit on a knuckle as they waited for a refrigerated truck.

'Don't run, it's suspicious,' Lucy warned, as it finally arrived and reversed into the loading dock.

'I'd feel safer with that,' Marion said, glancing at her bow on the rear seat.

'You any good?' Lucy asked.

'Can't manage Robin's fancy tricks, but I can shoot straight.'

As Marion said this, her aunt had a brainwave. Lucy leaned across from the driver's side and took a lipstick-sized stun gun out of the glove compartment.

'You shouldn't need it,' Lucy said. She pressed a button which set off a green charge indicator light. 'But better safe than sorry.'

'How do I use it?' Marion asked as she took the unit.

'Twist the base to arm. It fires twenty thousand volts when it touches something. It's not super powerful, but it will knock most people off their feet.'

Marion had put on a skirt and trainers because it would make her examination easier than boots and trousers. She dropped the stun gun into her top pocket as she got out of the car.

'They said it'll take an hour,' Marion said. 'I'll call if it's gonna be longer.'

Marion had sweated to the car seat with nerves, and shivered as an evening breeze hit the back of her dress. She walked briskly past new parents trying to fit a baby cradle in the back of their car and a line-up of old guys in hospital pyjamas, shivering and smoking.

Metal shutters had opened for the truck to unload, and two guys were wheeling wire trolleys stacked with clingfilm-covered breakfast trays.

'Maid?' a woman coming around the side of the truck asked, loud enough to make Marion jump.

The patient smuggling was a slick operation. As Marion walked behind the truck, a guy in a blue hospital porter smock tipped a large wheelie bin on its side.

His accent was Russian. 'I hosed most food scraps. You go in feet first.'

Marion slid into the bin, which had drips of water running down the inside. As her trainers touched sticky gunk in the bottom, the lid swung shut and she was plunged into darkness. Before she'd taken a breath the bin was upright, its twin rubber wheels rattling down a hospital corridor.

They were only at walking pace, but it seemed faster to Marion, with the little rubber wheels squeaking and every bump making the plastic boom like she was inside a drum.

'Sorry,' the orderly whispered, after a bump that made Marion's head whack the underside of the lid.

There were dirtier bins in the world, but the smell of raspberry yoghurt and gravy still made Marion queasy and she was grateful when her three-minute ride ended. The porter flipped the lid and helped Marion out in a store room containing a floor polisher and drums of cleaning products.

'I tell Chuma you're waiting,' the Russian said, as he pulled a metre of tissue from a dispenser and splashed it under a tap. 'You have stuck on your arm.'

Marion realised it was custard on the back of her arm and spotted the squashed peas on her kneecap. She considered wiping the gunk in the grips of her trainers, but Chuma arrived first.

'You made it,' Chuma said, cheerful and breathless.

He wore white Crocs, white trousers and a tight navy T-shirt with his hospital ID clipped on. He looked about twenty-five, with giant muscly arms and long hair in cornrows.

'Dr Chuma?' Marion said, deciding he was gorgeous.

'Not a doctor,' Chuma corrected. 'Just a lowly imaging technician.'

The hospital clinics were shut for the night, so there was a horror-movie vibe as they cut across an immensely long corridor with all the lights off. The sign on the room they entered read **Extremity Imaging**.

Three-quarters of the room was bare, apart from two plastic stacking chairs. At the far end was an oddly shaped recliner chair and a giant slab of machinery with a hole big enough for an arm or leg.

'What's the story?' Chuma asked.

'I was born with a club foot,' Marion explained. 'I had operations to straighten the foot when I was a toddler and wore a leg brace for ages. I've not had pain or anything, but Dr Gladys at Designer Outlets says the joint should

31

be scanned because I've grown a lot in the past couple of years.'

'Makes sense,' Chuma said. 'I'll look at your ankle in two different positions so we can see how the Achilles tendon moves. It's completely painless, though the MRI machine is noisy. Before we begin I'll need you to take everything off and put on a hospital gown.'

'I wore a skirt,' Marion said. 'If it's only my leg going in the machine, can't I just pull it up?'

Chuma shook his head. 'MRI stands for Magnetic Resonance Imaging,' he explained. 'When my machine is on, the magnets are powerful enough to throw an oxygen cylinder to the opposite side of this room. A tiny zip or an underwire in your bra could cause a serious injury when I turn the machine on. I'll get a basket for you to put your belongings in, then I'll set the imaging parameters in the control room while you change.'

'Right,' Marion said nervously.

Once she'd put on a disposable robe with the same texture as the tissue she'd used to wipe her arm, Chuma swept Marion with a handheld metal detector, then sat her on the recliner, which had a variety of positions and attachments for feeding limbs into the machine at different angles.

Marion felt self-conscious as the handsome medic fitted her operation-scarred foot and undersized calf muscle into a plastic brace. Then Chuma rolled the chair so that her leg got posted through the hole at the front of the machine.

'The computer says twenty-two minutes for each position,' Chuma warned. 'Keep still or I'll have to start again.'

As Chuma stepped on a lever to lock the wheels of the chair, he was startled by the sound of a door in the adjacent control room.

'Yoo-hoo,' a woman called. 'Anyone home?'

'Hang on,' Chuma told Marion, as he darted towards the control room. 'Can I help you?'

The chair was designed to hold Marion still, so she could only see the sides of the headrest if she turned. She felt anxious and vulnerable as she tried to understand muffled voices in the side room.

Finally, Chuma's voice blasted out from above and made Marion jump.

'What the?' Marion gasped as she realised there was a loudspeaker in the ceiling.

'Sorry,' Chuma said. 'It's loud so you can hear when the machine is running.'

'Everything OK?' Marion asked.

'Kaylee, the security guard. I accidentally left the side door open and she saw the light was on.'

'Is she trustworthy?' Marion asked.

'Kaylee is the best,' Chuma said reassuringly. 'I go to her summer barbecue every year. Her seven-layer dip is to die for.'

Marion managed a wry smile.

'Don't look so glum,' Chuma told her. 'Now, are you ready?'

'As I'll ever be.' Marion sighed.

# 7. BUTT PHONE CELL TOUR

Robin couldn't visit his dad in Pelican Island prison without getting busted, and prisoners weren't allowed to communicate with anyone who was wanted by the police. But now, Robin had a few precious minutes to speak with his dad.

'My biker friends smuggled the butt phone,' Ardagh explained. 'Most are basic phones, but this new one has a camera.'

'Did you say *butt* phone?' Robin asked.

'Prison slang,' Ardagh explained, his gentle tone reminding Robin of simpler times. 'Prisoners are strip searched when they arrive and after every visit. If you want to smuggle things in, you swallow them or stick them up your bum.'

'That's so gross!' Robin said, burying his face in his hands as Pauline and Little John laughed noisily.

'I hope you gave it a good wipe before you called,' Pauline howled.

Ardagh didn't like crude humour and looked uncomfortable.

'Want to tour my crib?' Ardagh asked, as he stood slightly and turned the camera into the cell. 'The bunks are so narrow I kept falling out of bed at first. Prison-issue pillows are filled with pinecones and razor blades, but my biker pals got me a better one.'

The camera glitched as Robin saw a metal sink and a sheet of polished metal that served as an unbreakable, but blurry, shaving mirror.

The wall opposite the bunks had a famous picture of Albert Einstein poking his tongue out, which belonged to Ardagh, and a larger poster of a girl in a swimsuit straddling a big motorbike, which definitely didn't.

Ardagh pointed the camera towards an enormous grey-bearded man, sitting on the top bunk near the cell's barred door, dressed in one sock and tartan boxer shorts.

'This is Joe,' Ardagh said. 'He's keeping watch along the balcony while I've got this phone out.'

'Is that your boy Robin?' Joe said, squinting as his puckered face closed on the tiny camera. 'I admire your chops, young man! I'm a tattooist and I've inked your name on a few arms since you got famous.'

Robin smiled. 'Have you given my dad any tats?'

Joe shook his head and laughed noisily, as Ardagh settled back in the corner with the camera.

'I was thinking of getting I ♥ Mozart on my arm,' Ardagh joked, before turning serious. 'Have you kept up with your studies?'

'Sure,' Robin said. 'We get lessons at Designer Outlets. Kids take exams and go off to university if they can get identity papers. Though it's madness right now. Loads of new kids at Designer Outlets because of the floods.'

'Studies are important,' Ardagh said dryly. 'I'm pleased Marjorie sent John to an excellent school.'

Robin didn't like talking about school and changed the subject. 'So you're doing OK?'

'I teach computer skills, like I did on the outside. The bikers make sure nobody hassles me. But there's zero privacy. On days when I'm not teaching, I spend twenty hours in this cell. I know you boys hate my cooking, but my lamb surprise is a gourmet treat compared to the slop they serve in here.'

Robin shuddered at the memory of lamb surprise. His dad made it by mixing minced lamb with leftovers and baking it dry.

'Auntie Pauline's doing a roast for my birthday,' Little John said. 'I'll bring brisket and birthday cake when I visit.'

'You must be careful,' Ardagh warned Robin. 'It's all fun and games robbing cash machines and getting in the news. But they'll throw away the key if they catch you.'

'I know, Dad,' Robin said, wishing his dad would be less of a downer. 'I learned my lesson after a few close scrapes. Will Scarlock and the rebels at Designer Outlets keep me on a tight leash.'

'Good,' Ardagh said, though even on a blurry web chat, Robin could tell his dad wasn't convinced.

'I hope you get to meet Will one day,' Robin said. 'You believe in all the same things.'

'Still got at least a year to serve,' Ardagh said, looking at the ceiling with sad eyes.

'Guard!' Joe shouted in the background.

'Time's up!' Ardagh said, making a half-salute, half-wave. 'I love you guys. Happy birthday, John, and I hope you enjoy Pauline's roast dinner.'

Everyone scrambled to say goodbye at once.

'Thanks, Dad,' Little John said. 'Love you.'

'I'll be up to visit on Thursday,' Pauline said.

'Hope we can do this again,' Robin said. 'Miss you loads.'

Then the laptop screen went black.

# 8. MAKING THE FINAL PAYMENT

Kaylee Portobello's rubber-soled shoes hardly made a sound as they padded along Locksley General's first floor. A name bounced around in the security guard's head as she pushed a door and stepped into the next section of hallway: *Marion Maid.*

The strip lights were triggered by motion sensors, with each bank of three flickering to life as Kaylee approached. This part of the hospital was all outpatient clinics, so the only people around on night shift were lost after visiting patients upstairs.

Kaylee knew that Chuma snuck patients in for imaging after hours and she'd gone into the control room out of boredom, hoping to break her twelve-hour shift with a chat.

The security guard almost wished she hadn't seen Marion's name on the imaging console's screen. She'd seen CCTV of Robin Hood and Marion Maid escaping on a dirt bike after their cash machine robbery trended everywhere.

Kaylee searched *Marion Maid* on her phone. The Locksley Police website said Guy Gisborne had put up a £30,000 reward for information leading to Marion Maid's capture.

Gisborne was a slimeball and she knew he'd weasel out of paying up. But Kaylee didn't need thirty thousand. She just needed one nasty lady off her back. So, loathing herself, but desperate to get out of a situation with very bad people, Kaylee unlocked the door of Locksley General's Anticoagulation Clinic, sat on a tatty waiting-room chair and dialled a number.

'Who this?' a shrill woman named Linda Brennan answered, as a quiz show blasted from her TV.

'It's Kaylee . . .'

'Got that seventeen hundred and fifty you owe me?'

'I have something else. Something better.'

Linda Brennan blew up. 'Pardon me? Pardon me?' she squawked. 'It's evening time, you understand? Got my glass of wine and my babies in bed. So if Kaylee Portobello is calling me, the *only* thing I want to hear is that she has seventeen fifty cash money and is on her way to drop it in my sweaty palm.'

'Please listen,' Kaylee begged. 'I don't have your money, but—'

'You're proper pissing me off!' Brennan raged. 'I told you you're getting done in if I don't see my money this week. Maybe I'll send Jayden and Owen out to pick your Jasprit up from school tomorrow. See how far she can swim when they chuck her in Macondo River.'

'If those yobs lay one hand on my daughter . . .' Kaylee hissed furiously.

'What?' Brennan laughed. 'You'll do what?'

'Listen for *one* minute,' Kaylee said. 'I know where Marion Maid is.'

'I have not the foggiest who that is.'

'Well, your boss Guy Gisborne does. Marion Maid is best pals with Robin Hood. I assume you've heard of *him*.'

Brennan snorted. 'You tripping if you think Gisborne will pay reward money.'

'That's true,' Kaylee said. 'But I've known you since school. You've spent years chasing a bigger taste of Gisborne's action. You fancy yourself the next Sheriff Marjorie, but you're a low-end loan shark working out of a mouldy flat and Guy Gisborne barely knows your name.'

'Keep disrespecting me and I'll have you sliced,' Brennan shouted.

Kaylee wished she hadn't started this, but made one final attempt to explain. 'If you deliver Marion Maid to Guy Gisborne, you will be his favourite person in the world. All I ask is that you wipe my debt.'

Kaylee realised she'd got through when Linda Brennan pressed mute on her TV.

'All right. Where?'

'You need to move fast,' Kaylee said. 'You need guys at Locksley General within twenty minutes. I can let them in through a window and take them to Marion Maid.'

Brennan made a weird growling noise then said, 'My lads will be there, but if you're wasting my time, that money you owe will be the least of your problems.'

# 9. EAT 'TIL YOU BURST

Robin pushed his chair back from the dining table as he swallowed a final mouthful of birthday cake.

'Soooo full,' he said, holding his belly.

The table was covered with dirty plates, and Pauline smiled proudly. 'Haven't got my own kids, so always a pleasure to feed you two.'

'Can I get your brisket recipe so the chefs at Sherwood Castle can make it?' Little John asked.

Robin didn't even have the energy to make a sarcastic comment about his brother being rich and having chefs. Auntie Pauline dodged the recipe request and started scraping plates, but John took them away.

'You were cooking all afternoon. Put your feet up. Me and the little squirt will clean up.'

'Good idea,' Robin agreed.

'Lovely,' Pauline said, as she took her glass of wine and rolled into the lounge area. 'Though I don't know what you two well-mannered boys have done with my nephews.'

Robin was surprised by the way his brother was acting. The Little John he'd grown up with would spend ten minutes trying to decide which shirt to put on. Apparently, seeing his dad thrown in jail, finding out that Sheriff Marjorie was his mother and getting sent to boarding school had made John grow up.

'Tough times in the forest right now,' Little John said as he scraped plates. 'You doing OK?'

'Floods ain't fun,' Robin said. 'And your mum's latest trick is sending Castle Guards out to set bear traps.'

John looked sceptical. 'Why would she do that?'

'Probably getting desperate,' Robin said. 'The hack I set up in the resort IT system is still live, so we know business is *way* down.'

'I live in the castle penthouse,' John told Robin as he rinsed out a roasting tin. 'When I go downstairs, the hotel and restaurants are dead. Your rebel pals attacking Mum's big game hunt scared people off. They've closed half the casino and there's not one wedding booked for spring.'

Robin gloated. 'Sheriff must be *furious*.'

Little John shrugged. 'A few months back, Sherwood Castle was raking profits in and my mum expected King Corporation to fund her bid to become president. Now, the castle is losing millions and people say Richard King III is about to fire her. But when I ask Mum if things are OK, she says it's all great.'

'Maybe she's nuts,' Robin suggested cheerfully as he stacked dessert bowls in the dishwasher. 'One of those people who acts normal – until they pull a gun and blast their brains out.'

Little John flashed with anger. 'She is my mum, you know.'

Robin glowered. 'She's a terrible person, who's hiring hundreds of new guards to attack Forest People.'

Pauline sensed tension between nephews and dived in.

'I've known Sheriff Marjorie since her first day at school,' Pauline said, as she parked her chair between the boys. 'Her brain runs six steps ahead of everyone else. And she's at her most dangerous when she's got her back to the wall.' Pauline locked eyes with Little John and spoke in a more soothing tone. 'We know Marjorie does bad things, but she's looked after you since your dad went to prison.'

John backed up to the fridge and sighed. 'I wish my life was less complicated!'

The sentiment chimed with Robin, who nodded and laughed.

'Marjorie's childhood was horrible,' Pauline said. 'Her mother was an addict, abusive stepdads, then bounced between foster homes. She'd turn up at school covered in bruises.'

'We're sure your mum is plotting something,' Robin told John. 'I guess it's up to you if you want to help us find out what that is.'

John looked offended. 'I saved your butt when you broke into the castle. You *know* whose side I'm on.'

Robin nodded. 'My hack into the castle's StayNet software gives us guest names and staff rotas, but we need to know what's in Sheriff Marjorie's head.'

'Did you bring the bugs and keylogger I asked for?' John asked.

'In my pack,' Robin said. 'I'll show you how to use them later.'

'Mum has an office below the castle penthouse,' Little John explained. 'She always used to work at the King Corporation building in Nottingham. But lately she's spending more time at the castle.'

'Can you get in her office?' Robin asked.

'I've yet to find an electronic lock at Sherwood Castle that my pass won't open,' John said. 'The only problem is Moshe Klein, my mum's head of security. He acts weird, like he suspects I'm feeding info back to you guys.'

'I can look at staff rotas and tell you when Moshe isn't working,' Robin suggested.

'Might help,' Little John agreed.

'Don't take silly risks,' Pauline warned. 'And this is all a bit serious for a family reunion. I brought a few board games. Birthday boy's choice.'

'Scrabble,' Little John said. 'I love it when I get a seven-letter word and Robin flings the board across the room.'

# 10. PINS AND NEEDLES

'Four minutes left,' Chuma told Marion as the MRI machine thumped. 'You did great at keeping still – the first scan is clean. I can't risk an email getting traced back to me, so I'll give you your scans on a memory card. But when you see Dr Gladys, tell her to bring my memory cards back with the next patient she sends. She must have twenty of 'em.'

'I will,' Marion said, as she tried to ignore the pain from her dead leg.

The first scan had been easy, but the second required a tight brace that pushed Marion's foot up, stretching her Achilles tendon. She wanted to keep the conversation with Chuma going to distract herself.

'So, you said you were a boxer?' Marion asked.

'In my misspent youth.' Chuma laughed. 'It's how I fell into this job. I was knocked out in a fight and needed a brain scan. Doctor said getting punched in the head was no way to make a living. I said, *What else am I gonna do?*

And the lady doing the scan says, *We're looking for trainee imaging technicians.'*

'Do you like the job?' Marion asked.

Chuma laughed. 'I get to dress like a doctor, but earn the same as the cleaners.'

'At least you're helping people,' Marion almost said.

But she only got two words out before a crash came through the speaker over her head.

'What the . . .'

The scanner stopped hammering and the next crash came with shouts and a sound like a mug breaking.

'Chuma?' Marion yelled anxiously.

Four thugs had burst into the little control room. They hadn't anticipated the imaging technician being a former cruiserweight boxer, but they knew it when Chuma punched one guy out and burst another's nose.

But Chuma was outnumbered. Another attacker picked up an office chair and used the wheeled base to pin him to the wall.

'Marion, run!' Chuma shouted as he battled the chair. 'Get out of there.'

That was easier said than done. The machine had stopped, but Marion had her leg strapped to a brace inside it. She put the heel of her free leg against the machine and tried to push the reclining chair backwards, but the wheels were locked so it grated against the floor.

After three hard shoves, Marion's braced leg was out of the scanner, but that didn't matter because an acne-scarred teen in a Macondo United shirt grabbed her under the arms and ripped her out of the chair.

'Got Maid,' he shouted keenly.

The brace wasn't designed for standing up, and its cuff dug painfully into Marion's heel as she tried to pull free. But her opponent was bigger and squashed Marion's face into the wall with a palm that stank of cigarettes. Then he used his other hand to pull her arm tight behind her back.

It sounded like the struggle with Chuma was over. An older guy came into the MRI room, grinning. He wore battered Nikes and a purple tracksuit, and had **KILLER** tattooed down the side of his massive neck.

'Nice work, boy,' Killer told the teen. Then menacingly to Marion, 'I bet Gisborne will try his whole whip collection out on you!'

'Up yours,' Marion snarled, but tears welled in her eyes as the brace cut into her heel and the teenager pulled her arm tighter.

'Let's get out of here,' the older guy said. 'Cops will steal our glory if we give 'em a chance.'

The teen flung Marion away from the wall, but the brace held her leg rigid, so she stumbled sideways and would have smacked the floor if he hadn't caught her.

'Get that thing off her leg,' Killer ordered.

A third man entered from the control room as the teen propped Marion back against the wall and began ripping the Velcro straps that held the leg brace.

'That doctor is strong as a bull,' the new arrival said breathlessly. 'Took three whacks on the head. Cuffed him to the desk and Carl's standing guard, but he's still fighting.'

As if to prove this point, a booming roar came out of the control room. Marion glanced through the room's slot window and saw that Chuma was back on his feet, wrestling his captor even though his hands were cuffed behind his back.

'You said you had him,' Killer roared furiously.

'He must have snapped the leg off the desk!'

'Go help Carl,' Killer said. Then to the teen, 'Stop gawping. Deal with that brace.'

Chuma's eyes bulged and his brow poured sweat. Marion assumed he'd try to escape the control room, but instead Chuma butted the scanner's control console, using his nose to switch the machine back on.

The instant the scanner resumed hammering, the powerful magnets inside hooked the thugs' keys, pocket change, belt buckles and phones. Since most items were attached or trapped in pockets, the three thugs in the scanner room got sucked to the machine like dirt up a vacuum cleaner.

The teen got the worst of it, knocked unconscious as his dental braces made him smash face-first into the front panel. Marion narrowly avoided Killer's purple-tracksuited leg as she dived to the floor.

When she looked back, Killer was trying to free himself by digging keys and coins out of his pocket, while the guy who'd just walked in moaned in agony. His back was against the scanner cabinet and his ribs were getting crushed as the magnets made the knife and phone in the front of his jacket into a powerful vice.

Marion ripped the last two straps off the brace and felt pins and needles up her leg as she kicked it free. A rubber cosh had fallen to the floor when the guys got thrown across the room, and she crawled forward to grab it.

She looked through an open door into the control room, hoping Chuma was OK. But while he'd flattened another guard, two more had stepped in to deal with him.

Marion thought about the basket with all her stuff in, but there was no way she could get into the control room without being seen, so she headed for the door.

The pins and needles still numbed her leg and her foot felt like a block of wood as she stepped into the hallway, hoping nobody was out there. Unfortunately, a pair of Linda Brennan's goons were less than two metres away.

One had taken Chuma's second punch and cradled a bloody nose and broken jaw. He was in no state to chase, but the other guy's trainers squealed on the polished hallway as he lunged at Marion.

She threw her body into a run, unsure if her dead leg would stand when she planted it. Her first couple of steps were awkward and she stumbled into the hallway wall, but she was soon running.

Marion was fast for a thirteen-year-old with a twisted foot, but her chunky red-faced pursuer almost had a hand on her paper gown as she smashed through a set of swinging doors.

The floor of the long hallway had lumps of plaster where a leak had brought down part of the ceiling. Marion yelped as a jagged chunk sliced her heel.

She had no idea which way led back to her aunt, because she'd arrived in a bin and hadn't seen a thing. But growing up in Sherwood had given Marion endurance. After almost getting caught, she'd gained thirty metres on her gasping pursuer as she blasted through another set of doors.

She'd reached a lobby at the end of the hallway. There were two lifts in front of her, both big enough to fit hospital beds. One had a half-open door and an *out of order* sign. To the right were stairs up and down. The down set had a *Hospital Staff Only* sign. Marion had to decide fast: she figured she was more likely to make it back to her auntie's car by going down than going up.

Marion also realised she had a fifty-fifty chance of the guy on her tail going the wrong way if she vanished before he came through the swinging doors. She hopped on a banister and slid down, and since it was fast and silent, she went around the landing and slid down the next flight too.

Marion pushed through a tatty door at the bottom of the stairs and glanced back, but could see no obvious way to lock it. Green emergency exit signs gave the only light, but two steps triggered strip lights leading to another set of doors fifty metres away.

The hallway upstairs had been wide enough for patients in wheeled beds to pass. Here it was barely the width of two bodies, with paint that hadn't been refreshed in the hundred years since Locksley General opened, and rusty pipes along the ceiling.

Bare feet and the paper gown made Marion feel vulnerable, and it didn't help that this was exactly the kind of dank hallway where people get murdered in horror movies.

As Marion jogged, she passed alcoves which had waste chutes above. Some chutes dropped into giant rubbish bins. Other alcoves were piled with mounds of soiled bed linen or bright orange drums with biohazard labels.

Marion looked into each alcove, hoping to find the door or shutter through which the rubbish got taken out. She hopped over a puddle below a dripping pipe and when she glanced back, had the horrible realisation that her wounded heel was trailing red smudges.

When she heard footsteps coming off the stairs behind, Marion considered hiding in an alcove, or laying ambush and whacking the guy with the cosh she'd picked up. But she didn't like the idea of being trapped and made a sprint for the doors at the far end.

She realised there were two sets of footsteps. The guy who'd been chasing her before was slow and held his gut like he had a stitch. But it seemed that Killer had shed enough metal from his purple tracksuit to escape the clutches of the MRI machine, and his hair brushed the ceiling pipes as he ran flat out.

More lights flicked on as Marion passed through double doors into the next section of the basement hallway. She got a blast of heat as she passed a boiler room with a padlock and chain on the door, then hit the next set of doors. She expected them to swing like the others, but almost knocked herself out when they didn't budge. There was a light shining under the door and a clattering inside – maybe a printer or tumble dryer.

'Help!' Marion screamed as she pounded desperately on the door. 'Please let me in.'

She turned away from the door as Killer booted ferociously through the last set of swinging doors. Marion gripped the rubber cosh, but the guy's fists were as big as her head and she knew she had zero chance if he got hold of her.

# 11. ZITS AND GOSSIP

The swanky eighth-floor student apartment had two bedrooms with en-suite bathrooms. After showing her nephews who was boss by smashing them in three games of Scrabble, Pauline headed off to the master bedroom, while the boys retired to single beds she'd set up in the other one.

Little John was towelling off after a shower. His huge frame left little space in the bathroom for Robin, who stood at the sink brushing his teeth.

'Can you remember when we last shared a bedroom?' Little John asked.

'Maybe a camping trip with Dad,' Robin said, then gasped as blobs of toothpaste dribbled down his new shirt. 'Balls!'

John smiled. 'I laugh about camping now, but it was properly miserable!'

'Always rained,' Robin agreed. 'So what did you tell your mum about tonight?'

'Mate from school's sleepover,' Little John explained as he unzipped a wash bag and took out his toothbrush. 'You done?'

Robin backed up to the door leading into their bedroom, but gasped as Little John leaned over the sink.

John looked baffled. 'What?'

Robin snorted. 'Your back has the biggest zit *ever*. It's like you're growing a second head.'

John cleared a patch on the steamed-up mirror and reached around to feel his back.

'They shoot like bombs when you squeeze 'em,' John said, locating the monster zit.

To prove his point, he turned his back towards Robin and squashed the zit.

'You're revolting!' Robin yelled as he backed out of the doorway, laughing.

John kept backing up towards Robin, who had no idea that his brother wasn't squeezing the zit hard enough to pop it.

'I'll show mercy,' John teased, as he walked back to the bathroom. 'This time . . .'

Robin was laughing too hard to see his brother's jeans in the middle of the floor. He hooked his toes in the waistband and stumbled face-first over John's bed.

'It was such a good evening.' Robin smiled, rolling onto his back and staring at the ceiling. 'Hanging out with no hassles.'

As John started brushing his teeth, his phone bleeped on his bedside table, close to where Robin was lying. Robin couldn't see the whole message but the opening lines showed in a bubble on the screen:

> **Clare Gisborne**
> **Missed you today. Can't wait to give you your birthday kiss when we ...**

Robin gawped at the message for several seconds before deciding what to do.

'How's it going with Clare Gisborne these days?' he asked casually.

'We have some classes together,' John said, then after a pause to gargle and spit, 'She's nice once you get to know her, and we have loads in common. Like, we both got sent to Barnsdale School at the same time and we both have messed-up power-hungry parents.'

'So, just mates?' Robin said, as he got off the bed holding his brother's phone.

'Exactly.'

Robin struggled to keep a straight face as he held up the phone. 'So why did Clare send you a message, saying she can't wait to give you a birthday kiss?'

Still with toothpaste down his chin, John exploded out of the bathroom and tried to snatch the phone. 'That's private!' he sputtered. 'Give!'

Robin stood on the bed, singing, 'Gisborne is your girlfriend. Gisborne is your girlfriend!'

As John tried to sweep his legs away, Robin hopped across to his own bed.

It was a battle the brothers had played out a thousand times, John big and strong, Robin small and nimble.

Unfortunately for Robin, Barnsdale rugby training had made John faster than expected and he wrapped an arm around Robin's knees. Unfortunately for John, Robin had been working out with weights. This made Robin stronger than expected and he broke free, clutching his brother's phone as he scrambled away.

John blocked the main door, so Robin headed for the bathroom.

'I know how to hack your log-in,' Robin teased, snorting with laughter. 'I'll message Clare and say you spent your birthday snogging another girl.'

As Robin hit the bathroom tiles, he spun and tried to slam the door. But John was too fast and barged it with his shoulder.

'Now where you gonna go?' John grinned, as he filled the doorway.

Robin expected his brother to lunge for the phone, but in a shock move John effortlessly lifted Robin off the floor and drove him backwards into the shower tray.

'Think you need another wash,' John said.

'Your phone will get wet!' Robin yelped desperately.

'Water-resistant,' John said cockily, as he turned the shower to full-blast cold.

'Take the phone!' Robin yelled. 'It's freezing.'

'Tell me what a great brother I am first,' John said, batting Robin's hands away from the tap.

Robin didn't want to give his brother the satisfaction, but the water was freezing and he could hardly breathe.

'You're a great brother,' he growled.

'Just great, or the greatest?' John asked, then jumped out of his skin as Pauline yelled right behind him.

'Pack it in, you two!'

As Pauline scowled from the doorway, John spun around. Robin reached up and switched off the cold blast.

'You're worse than a pair of five-year-olds,' Pauline said. She tried to sound furious, but Robin shivering with water pouring out of his tangled hair and Little John in his undershorts with toothpaste down his face was too much for her to keep a straight face.

'Sorry, Auntie,' Robin said, not sounding terribly sincere. 'Let me hug you better!'

John thought this was a great idea, and let Robin out of the bathroom. Pauline yelped and reversed her chair as Robin came at her, dripping cold water.

'I'm cold, Auntie. Warm me up!'

'Don't you dare,' Pauline howled as Robin closed in. 'If I get wet, I'll write the pair of you out of my will!'

# 12. WHEN YOU LEAST EXPECT IT

Killer was less than three metres away, and Marion had her back so hard against the door that she fell inside when it opened.

'What the deuce!' a woman in green scrubs said, then yelped, 'No, no, no!' when she saw Killer about to smash into her.

Marion fell sideways onto sticky carpet tiles. As she found her balance, she realised she was in a staff break room, with microwaves, coffee machine and battered chairs. There were eight or nine people spread about, and the crashing door and the appearance of a girl in a paper robe made most of them stand to see what was happening.

The woman who'd opened the door took a brutal hit from Killer, as did a smartly dressed hospital administrator.

'Stop and we'll help you,' a nurse told Marion, as the teenager scrambled towards stairs going up at the far side of the staff lounge.

As Marion took the stairs two at a time, a cop who worked in the lobby stumbled out of a toilet cubicle, pulling her blouse straight then reaching for the gun in her belt. The first thing she saw was Killer, charging across the staff lounge with people backing out of his path.

'Police, halt!' Marion heard, but it wasn't directed at her, and she kept going up.

'Final warning!'

As Killer reached the bottom of the stairs, a deafening blast ripped across the staff lounge. People screamed and Marion's ears rang, as Killer dived and a bullet blew chunks out of plaster out of the wall.

'I warned you,' the cop shouted as she closed Killer down. 'Do not move a muscle.'

The bullet had missed, but plaster chunks clogged Killer's ear and cut his cheek.

'That was Marion Maid,' Killer growled, pointing up the stairs.

He looked nervous, because Locksley cops had a 'shoot first and ask questions later' reputation. Especially when you were a guy with prison tattoos on your neck.

'Robin Hood's number-one associate,' Killer continued. 'Gisborne sent me after her and *you* let her go.'

Killer hadn't been sent by Gisborne, but he knew Gisborne controlled the Locksley Police department, and that cops who got in the gangster's way got framed or fired.

'Marion who?' the cop asked, keeping her gun aimed at Killer as she stepped closer.

'She rode the bike with Robin Hood in that robbery video,' Killer growled, as he flicked plaster out of his bloody ear.

'You need to arrest this creep, Susan,' a nurse told the cop.

'Take all the time you need,' Killer told the cop mockingly. 'It's not like Marion Maid is running away or anything . . .'

'Susan,' the nurse repeated. 'He sent Lupita flying and Mitchell's got a split lip.'

The cop didn't trust Killer but didn't want to risk upsetting Gisborne either.

'Hands where I can see 'em,' the cop warned, reaching for the radio hooked to her shirt. 'This is a code seven-two,' she told the radio. 'Repeat, seven-two. Suspect description: Marion Maid. Female, early teens, wearing a hospital gown. Looks like she's barefoot and bleeding.'

By this time, Marion had bolted up two flights of stairs and exited into a high-ceilinged atrium with a ripe smell of floor polish. The gunshot had confused and frightened her, but at least nobody had followed her upstairs.

A coffee counter and newsagent were closed for the night, and a few people sat on benches. Beyond this area was the modern security lobby with the cops and X-ray machines.

This was the exact part of the hospital Marion had been trying to avoid, though it worked in her favour that it was Saturday night. There were loads of people trying to enter the hospital, and cops on the security counters were getting abuse from the drunk and drugged. Others had minor injuries, and a large family group swarmed one counter demanding to be let in.

'Our papa is dying,' a man shouted as he kicked a counter. 'I have no identity card because I ran out to be with the ambulance.'

Everyone seemed too wrapped up in their own business to notice Marion. Since the security get-up was designed to stop patients and visitors from getting in, she made a quick study and thought there might be a way out.

Three cops manned three security desks with X-ray machines, there was a supervisor with sergeant's stripes in a booth, and more desks that were cordoned off. To the left of this area was a separate entrance with swinging waist-height gates where ambulance crews delivered patients on trolleys.

Rather than a cop, this area was staffed by a bored-looking hospital employee. She had a crazy bleached Afro, white earbuds, and played a game on her phone. Marion hoped she could sprint across the floor and hurdle the gates before the guard even looked up.

Someone might chase, but Aunt Lucy had driven past the lobby on the way in, so Marion knew where she was and reckoned she could run to her aunt's car in less than forty seconds.

She felt sick with fear, but the longer Marion waited, the more chance she'd get spotted. As she started her run, she noticed the cops on the security desks gathering around their supervisor.

'Code seven-two,' the sergeant shouted through the hall. 'Lockdown!'

Marion sprinted over the yellow striped floor of the ambulance zone as the sergeant slammed the emergency button under a desk. The green lights over the X-ray gates turned red and the people queuing got louder.

'Emergency, nobody in or out!' one cop yelled.

'Stay behind the line!' another added, as people piled up around his counter.

As Marion shot past, the bored guard at the ambulance counter looked up from her game and blinked in shock. A siren erupted, along with blue lights around the lobby exterior. The flashes dazzled Marion as she vaulted the low gates, but to her horror the lockdown had activated a drop-down grille on the outside.

She considered making a dive and rolling under before it shut, but didn't get close.

'Damn!' she hissed as she clattered into the grille.

As Marion looked back towards the lobby, she saw the guard stride purposefully from behind the counter. She wore the dark green uniform of the Locksley Ambulance Service. No older than twenty and no taller than Marion. Her trousers were tucked into crazy yellow basketball boots with a fur trim.

Marion thought about running, but the guard's voice was friendly. 'I know you,' she said, having to yell over the sirens.

After a sly glance to make sure none of her colleagues were looking, the guard pulled an emergency override lever that made the metal shutter start rising again.

'You saved my life,' Marion gasped, before there was a space big enough to squeeze through.

'Good luck,' the guard said as Marion crawled under the barrier towards the flashing blue lights. 'When you see Robin Hood, tell him I said hi.'

# 13. ZEBRAS FLOATING BY

'Hardly slept last night,' Robin complained, as he grabbed a monster pack of two hundred and eighty disposable nappies from the back of a panel van. 'Little John's snore is like spending the night with a tuba.'

Marion smiled, then winced at the pain that shot up her leg as she dragged out an identical box of nappies.

'Sit in the van if it hurts,' Robin said. He started down a steep canal bank with the vast but lightweight pack blocking his view. It was first light, with slippery cobbles underfoot, though for once it had stopped raining.

'Agony getting my boot on,' Marion said. 'But it's not bad now it's on.'

'And what happened after the security person let you escape?' Robin asked, as Marion walked behind.

'Aunt Lucy was snoring her head off,' Marion explained, shaking her head. 'Sirens were going off, blue flashing lights everywhere, and I'm banging on the car window trying wake her up. The car park exit was blocked, so I took my bow and a pair of flat shoes Aunt Lucy keeps in the car and we snuck away from the hospital on foot.'

Robin nodded. 'It's desolate around Locksley General.'

They both backed into weeds at the side of the cobbled path, so that Lyla and eighteen-year-old rebel Neo Scarlock could pass in the other direction.

'We jogged for a couple of kilometres,' Marion said, continuing her story as they started walking again. 'One of Lucy's friends picked us up, and I slept on the sofa at her place. Good job we didn't go back to Aunt Lucy's. They kicked her apartment door in at three this morning. Threw stuff around and made threats to her partner, Seb.'

'Did he give anything away?'

Marion laughed. 'Lucy called Seb to say we were safe, but she wasn't stupid enough to tell him where we were.'

'I activated the remote wipe software I put on the phone you lost,' Robin said. 'So cops won't get any information off that.'

'It's Chuma I feel bad for,' Marion said. 'He got battered by thugs, then Lucy's friend at the hospital said cops arrested him for stealing medical equipment and aiding refugees. Lucy asked our lawyer, Tybalt, to go to Central Police Station and help him out, but he's in serious trouble.'

Robin shook his head in disgust as they reached the end of the path and the bank of a broad canal. The waterway had been built to ferry rolled steel to Locksley's biggest car plant, but now the plant was bulldozed and the canal was an obscure mooring spot used by smugglers and Forest People.

Water glinted in the first morning sun. Their open-hulled boat was half-filled with supplies.

'Hope we can fit everything in,' Robin said, as he dumped the nappies in the boat. 'There's still heaps up in the van.'

Marion nodded as they heard Neo and Lyla coming with more supplies. 'Wouldn't be the first time I've ridden upriver squashed between sacks of spuds,' she said.

They made three more round trips to the dock before the van was empty. Lyla said Gisborne's thugs took more interest in boats with valuable cargo than in ones arriving empty, so she was keen to hit open water while the criminal community enjoyed their Sunday lie-in.

Neo said goodbye and left with the van, but as they were about to board the boat, Lyla sensed something she didn't like.

'Get the two boxes of medicine and the computer gear off the boat,' Lyla ordered urgently as she felt vibrations in the canal wall.

'Surge from upriver?' Marion asked, noticing the mud swirling in the dock water.

'Feels like it.' Lyla nodded.

'Doesn't the Water Authority send a warning?' Marion asked, as Robin grabbed bows and packs out of the boat.

'They're supposed to,' Lyla said. 'But it doesn't always happen.'

Robin, Lyla and Marion worked quickly. There wasn't time to completely empty the boat but they carried personal belongings and the most valuable cargo up the cobbled path to higher ground. By the time they took the last loads, choppy brown water was lapping over the bank, and distant boats sounded warning blasts on their fog horns.

'You'll get a view from the top of the embankment,' Lyla said. 'Surges can be spectacular.'

Robin and Marion reached a section of pathway with a view along the river. The Macondo was over a hundred metres wide, and the only traffic in view was two little pleasure boats and a tug pulling four barges mounded with compacted trash.

'Will they sink?' Robin asked, shielding his eyes from the low sun.

'A surge feels like a bump if you're on open water,' Lyla explained, as the rumbling grew louder. 'But if we'd been caught leaving the dock, or near the riverbank, the surge could slam the boat into a wall and splinter us.'

More horns made an eerie chorus along the river as the rush of churning water got loud. Robin and Marion jolted backwards as a huge tree trunk smashed into the riverbank less than ten metres away.

'Look at them go,' Marion said, as the little pleasure boats rocked violently.

The garbage barges bobbed dramatically, and down in the canal their little boat scraped along the wall as spray blasted up the banks.

After the surge it got quiet, but the river churned silt and slower-moving debris. Floating dustbins, a car bonnet and birds looking for dead fish.

'Zebra!' Marion shouted, pointing to the far side of the river.

Robin assumed it was her weird sense of humour, until he saw a flat-bedded metal raft designed to take cars across narrower parts of the river. The raft had broken its mooring, and a confused zebra stood on its loading bed.

'Poor thing,' Marion said.

'Must be one of the ones that escaped when that truck crashed on Route 24,' Robin said.

Lyla sounded thoughtful. 'If zebras are like horses, it will swim to shore when it gets to calmer water in the delta.'

Robin wasn't a confident swimmer, and was glad they'd missed the swell as Marion led the way back down the canal side. Their boat was listing and several packages had floated out towards the far side of the canal.

'Could have been worse,' Lyla said, as her phone gave a notification ping. 'I told Neo to make sure all the packages were waterproof. We can bail out and there won't be another surge for a day or two.'

Lyla took her phone out, then stamped furiously as she read a message.

'They deliberately send these notices out late to mess with Forest People,' Lyla spat, showering her phone in spit.

'What's up?' Robin asked

Lyla turned her phone so Robin and Marion could read for themselves.

EMERGENCY NAVIGATION NOTICE
Due to high water levels caused by recent
Level 5 flooding, Sherwood Dam No. 1 (Darley
Dale) and Sherwood Dam No. 4 (Bolsover) will
stage an emergency release of water between
0603 and 0619 on Sunday 10th October.

This event is designed to prevent upstream
flooding and the contamination of drinking
water.

Vessels below 50 tonnes could be endangered
by a surge and are advised to seek sheltered
mooring by 0600.

# 14. TERRIFIC EXAMPLE OF PRIMITIVISM

Little John got up at seven every weekday at boarding school, so he tried to lie in until at least eleven on Sundays. But Robin disturbed him when he left at quarter to six and Pauline made more racket vacuuming and emptying the dishwasher. So John helped his aunt carry her cooking stuff and leftover food down to her car, then used the King Corporation account to book a limo back to Sherwood Castle.

He called Clare Gisborne as he sat in the back of a black Mercedes heading out of Locksley towards Route 24.

'Hello, you,' Clare said fondly, as she cracked a yawn.

'You in bed?'

'It's Sunday – of course I'm in bed. You?'

'I wish.' John laughed.

'How was last night?' Clare asked.

John liked Clare a lot, but he hadn't told her about the secret meeting with Robin.

'Birthday meal with my mum,' he lied. 'You?'

'Watched junk TV with my brothers. Mum and Dad screamed at each other as usual and . . .'

The line went quiet, and John wondered if the call had dropped.

'Aaaaand,' Clare repeated, sounding cross.

John couldn't work out why Clare was angry, but knew she shared her father Guy Gisborne's vile temper.

'Did I do something wrong?' he asked meekly.

'I was going on about it *all* week,' Clare said. 'Saturday morning, half past eleven. Left school early on Friday so I could do extra practice with my instructor . . .'

'Driving test,' John blurted, sounding like he'd got the jackpot question on a quiz show. 'How did it go?'

'Passed, *obviously*,' Clare said.

'Nice!'

'I was sure I'd failed. The instructor said turn right, but there was a truck in the way and I didn't see the turning. He said it just cost me a mark, but I scraped through.'

John laughed. 'Poor examiner was probably terrified of your dad. You could have mown down statues in Central Square and he still would have passed you.'

'Bog off!' Clare said, as she thumped her mattress. 'I passed like everyone else.'

'Sorry,' John said, stifling a laugh. 'I had a mental image of a driving test examiner being found frozen solid in a meat locker.'

73

'You're a dick sometimes,' Clare moaned. 'You could just say well done, like a normal person.'

John moved the subject along as his ride pulled off a slip road and accelerated onto Route 24. 'So, you getting a car?'

'Dad's letting me use Mum's old Lexus. It's tatty, but Dad says he's not getting me anything newer until I'm more experienced.'

'A five-year-old Lexus isn't the end of the world,' John pointed out. 'It's frustrating not seeing you all weekend. I've decided to crack on with my History coursework when I get home. Get the whole essay done in one boring day. Then I'll never have to think about Napoleon's Siege of Manchuria again.'

'Sounds thrilling,' Clare said dourly. 'My soccer is cancelled because the pitches are waterlogged. I might go and practise my skillz in the Lexus. Take my little brothers for tacos, or something.'

'We'll celebrate properly next Saturday,' John said. 'My birthday and your driving test.'

'Good idea,' Clare said, then blurted, 'Damn . . . gotta go.'

'You OK?' Little John asked.

'Mum and Dad went to buy bathroom tiles. I'm supposed to be watching my brothers and it sounds like they're about to kill each other.'

'See you at school tomorrow.'

'Birthday kisses,' Clare said. 'Haven't forgotten!'

There was no traffic, and half an hour later John stepped out of the lift into Sherwood Castle's penthouse. He was surprised to see his mum, Sheriff Marjorie, in the wide marble-clad hallway. Her entire art collection was down off its hooks and two maintenance staff held up a huge painting that Little John hadn't seen before.

'Morning, son,' Marjorie said fondly.

John got his bulk from his mother, making her the only person he knew who didn't have to go on tiptoes to kiss his cheek.

'Good party with the boys from school?' Marjorie asked, as she sniffed John's shirt. 'Can't smell drugs or booze, so it can't have been too wild.'

'It was decent,' John said, faking a yawn. 'I need a nap, though. Didn't get to sleep until three.'

'Before you hide in your room for the rest of the day, what do you think of the Twombly?'

The two men holding up the picture strained as John inspected the giant canvas. It had black splodges along the top and a scribble like a four-year-old's drawing of a ball of string.

'I think it's less hideous than the Picasso octopus lady,' Little John said. 'The massive one by the guy who threw paint around is still my fave.'

'I should sign you up for art appreciation class.' Marjorie laughed. 'Cy Twombly was one of the great twentieth-century primitivists. This is his best work to come up at auction in years.'

John shook his head. 'If you say so, Mum.'

'I thought it would go in the spot left by the Picasso I sold. But it didn't look right and then I started moving all the other pictures around . . .'

John fake-yawned and pointed towards his bedroom door. 'I'm *really* tired.'

'I'm glad you had a good time,' Marjorie said. 'I worried you wouldn't fit in at your new school.'

John opened a door into a spectacular bedroom, with an emperor-size bed and floor-to-ceiling glass, giving views down to the forest canopy. Every day John's towels and bedding got changed, every surface was scrubbed, and even tiny details like a squeaky hinge or a dead fly inside a light fixture were swiftly dealt with.

If John threw dirty clothes on the floor, they came back a day later, pressed and wrapped in tissue paper, and chefs would prepare any dish he ordered, even at 3am.

John felt guilty about this lavishness when he only had to look out of the window to see the forest, where people were drowning in mudslides and kids drank water loaded with parasites. But he also found the five-star lifestyle addictive.

He was thinking about a soak in his jet bath and the steak with truffle mashed potato he'd order before starting on his history coursework when his mum knocked on the door.

'Sorry, I know you're tired,' Marjorie said, poking her head around the door. 'I forgot to say, I'm flying off to

Capital City for a TV interview. But since I haven't seen you all week, maybe we can eat dinner together around eight o'clock?'

John nodded enthusiastically. 'I want to power through my History coursework, so that's perfect.'

Marjorie gave a cheery thumbs-up as she backed out.

'And give the interviewer hell,' John shouted after her.

# 15. GOD-LEVEL PIE

Marion and Robin got wet fishing spilled cargo from the dock, and wetter when they bailed out the listing hull. There were no dry places to sit. By the time Lyla piloted the little boat out onto the Macondo River, the rising sun was curtained by slate-grey clouds.

Lightning flashed as the boat went at full speed, skimming past flooded waterfront houses.

'This is nuts,' Robin complained. Blobs filled his eyes faster than he could blink as he scooped rainwater into a bucket and flung it over the side.

The teens couldn't shelter under the tarp they'd used the day before because Lyla had tied it over the cargo to stop stuff moving around. She had it even tougher, steering the outboard motor and squinting through the rain to see where she was going.

Marion found the closest thing to a dry spot by squashing into a gap between the giant packs of nappies.

She wore her big floppy rain hat as she checked her messages on Robin's phone.

'You OK?' Robin asked, as he crawled over the nappies.

He wasn't bothered about puddled water, because his clothes couldn't get any wetter.

Marion's huge blue eyes had struck Robin the first time he met her. Now they had a frightened look that he'd not seen before.

'Aunt Lucy sent a message,' Marion said sadly. 'They've seized the white car and her flat is wrecked. Cops broke the bathroom sink, ripped doors off kitchen cabinets and stomped food into her carpets.'

'Animals,' Robin said.

'That's not the worst of it,' Marion said. 'Tybalt visited Chuma at the police station. The detectives are threatening to throw the book at him. Ten years' jail, unless he rats out everyone at Locksley General who's been helping us.'

Robin looked angry. 'He'd better not. Grasses get battered in prison.'

'Chuma's a nice guy with three little kids,' Marion snapped. 'Last night was the worst thing ever . . .'

She sobbed. Robin hardly believed he'd heard it, because she was tough and acted tougher.

'Hey,' Robin said soothingly, as he shoved the nappies away so he could slide down beside her.

Marion was furious that she'd let Robin see she was upset. She tried telling him to bog off and find his own dry spot, but only sobs came out.

'It sucks,' Robin soothed, slipping an arm around Marion's shuddering back. 'But we'll keep fighting, like we always do.'

'I can't stop thinking about last night,' Marion sniffed. 'If Chuma hadn't turned the MRI back on, they would have got me. If the woman hadn't opened the staffroom, they would have got me. If the guard hadn't let me through the gate . . . It's a miracle that I'm here, not tied up in Gisborne's basement getting whipped.'

'I'm surprised Gisborne went after you,' Robin said. 'Your dad is boss of the baddest biker gang in the county. Harming you would mean war between Gisborne and the bikers.'

'Gisborne's a psycho,' Marion said. 'That nut probably wanted a war.'

'Maybe those people weren't sent by Gisborne,' Robin suggested. 'They could have been after the reward.'

Marion found a pack of pocket tissues and used one to dab her eyes.

'And this is all *your* fault, Robin Hood,' she growled.

Robin looked aghast as he loosened his grip on Marion's shoulder. 'How'd you figure that?'

'Before I met you, I was a random forest kid nobody'd ever heard of,' Marion explained. 'Now I'm Marion Maid, sidekick of Robin Hood, with a bounty on my head.'

Another lightning blast ripped across the sky. Marion slid her head into Robin's lap then looked up at him, smiling.

'That one was a monster!' Lyla shouted from the back of the boat. 'Looks like we're heading straight into the worst of it.'

'I don't really blame you,' Marion said, red-eyed and slightly smiling. 'You've never forced me into anything.'

Robin had never seen Marion cry before, and she was the last person he'd expected to plonk their head in his lap. He didn't rule out the possibility it was a trick to give him a nipple cripple or a slap in the nuts, but the weirdest part was he could feel Marion's breath and wanted to kiss her.

Marion also caught the odd vibe.

*I bawled in front of Robin. Now I've got my head in his lap. He looks scared of me, but he's also adorable with rain pouring down his stupid face and . . . WHAT AM I THINKING!*

Marion sat up so fast, Robin almost got a headbutt.

'I feel weird because I didn't sleep or eat breakfast,' she blurted. 'My mums say it's the most important meal of the day.'

Keen to escape the awkwardness, Robin clambered over the cargo to get his backpack.

'If you're hungry you'll love this,' he said, as he unzipped and pulled out a plastic tub. Pauline had cut the pear and custard tart into twelve triangular slices, each sealed in a bag with a disposable bamboo fork.

She'd also sent a note, with two handwritten lines and a drawing:

*Share this with Marion and her family!*
*Don't be a . . .*

Auntie Pauline was a talented cartoonist. Robin smiled at her drawing of a curly-tailed pig.

He handed a bagged slice to Marion. The rain blasted their cargo as he crawled to the back of the boat and offered another slice to Lyla. She took the tart and, since she was steering, she asked him to pour coffee from her flask. By the time Robin returned, Marion had settled back in the gap between the nappies. She didn't exactly look happy, but her cheeks were stuffed with pie.

'This is God-level pie,' Marion told Robin, as she swallowed. 'I command you to get the recipe off your aunt so my mums can make it.'

Robin grabbed a slice and sat on the nappies above Marion. 'Pear and custard was my favourite,' he explained. 'I'd ask for this instead of birthday cake.'

'Did I see Lyla with hot coffee?' Marion asked, cracking her cheekiest smile.

'She's got a flask.'

'Well, since you're already on your feet . . .'

'I just sat down.' Robin tutted. 'You don't even like coffee.'

'It goes with pie,' Marion said. 'Especially when it's hot and I'm shivering.'

'You'll be colder when I tip the bail-out bucket over your head,' Robin said, but he did the decent thing and crawled off to get Lyla's flask.

# 16. THE THIRTY-MARK ESSAY

Little John put his lunch tray out in the hallway so he wasn't disturbed when the kitchen staff came to collect it. He dressed in his comfiest tracksuit, put his laptop, textbooks, notes and highlighter pens on his desk, then made sure his phone was on silent and left it in the drawer beside his bed so that he wasn't tempted to mess with it.

'Let's do this,' John told himself, cracking his knuckles and starting to read the essay instruction sheet:

> This essay is worth thirty marks in your final assessment. You must write three or four main arguments and provide historical proof for each point raised. The conclusion must synthesise your core arguments, using them to explain the conclusion you have reached, while simultaneously . . .

'I hate my life!' John groaned, thinking about the boring hours that lay ahead as he sat with his nose squashed against his desk.

And tomorrow was Monday, which meant getting up super early to be at Barnsdale School by seven-thirty. Then five whole days of school and . . .

*When you've written the first argument, you can call the kitchen and order chocolate brownies.*

But before John could start writing, he had to figure out what his arguments were going to be. An hour later, he had several scrunched-up essay plans, one badly written paragraph, and realised he needed to read more source material for his essay to be any good.

The bedroom door clicked, snapping John out of his study coma.

'Oh, Mr Kovacevic!' Pia the maid said as she charged in. 'So sorry! I thought you were away.'

John liked Pia, and was grateful for any distraction from the essay. 'How was your day off?' he asked. 'You said you were going shopping with your sister.'

'Very good,' Pia said. 'I got Christmas things to send to my nephews in Manila. I can clean later when you are not here, but may I take laundry now?'

'You can get the wet towels out of the bathroom, and there are some clothes I wore yesterday in the overnight bag.'

John imagined flinging his History textbooks off the penthouse balcony as Pia scooped up his dirty robe and used a wet towel to rub drips from his shower screen.

'Can I go inside your bag?' Pia asked, as she came out.

'No worries,' John said

But as Pia headed for the backpack, he remembered that the surveillance gear Robin gave him was in there.

'Actually . . .' Little John blurted, rolling back his chair and swiping the bag before Pia got to it.

As the maid headed out with an armful of laundry, John took a metal pencil tin from the pack and opened it to reveal a pair of listening devices and a memory card onto which Robin had loaded hacking software.

Since Marjorie had flown to Capital City and John would be at boarding school all week, it would be six days before he got another chance to go in his mum's downstairs office. Robin had yet to check the StayNet system and let him know when security chief Moshe Klein was off duty, but John had thought up an excuse for going in his mum's office.

The office had a large-format printer. John's idea was to download the most detailed Napoleonic battle map he could find, then set it to print out in his mum's office. If he got caught in the office, he'd say the map was to help with his essay and it was better on a big sheet.

After finding a suitable map online and setting it to print poster-size, John left the apartment, crossed the lift lobby and took the curving marble stairs down one floor.

The seventh floor had Sherwood Castle Resort's most lavish function rooms. These could be booked for wedding receptions or meetings, but since it was a Sunday and resort business was bad there was nobody around.

After swiping his security pass, John stepped into his mother's office. The window at the far end had a good view over the forest, but it lacked the penthouse floor's double-height ceilings. The furnishings were basic, with file boxes stacked on metal racking, a fire safe, two grey desks and a wall lined with office equipment.

John saw his giant map waiting in the printer tray, but his eyes were drawn to an architect's model of Sherwood Castle that hadn't been in the room when he'd come down to get a school permission slip signed a couple of weeks earlier.

The listening device was his top priority. It was the size and thickness of a credit card, and Robin had preconfigured it to join Sherwood Castle's public Wi-Fi.

Its voice-activated microphone would record anything Marjorie said and store it on a memory chip. Once a day, the device would email Robin a compressed sound file. Because the bug only transmitted for a few seconds each day, it was virtually impossible to detect and it would work for several months before the battery died.

John figured the best spot was the underside of his mother's desk. Robin had provided disposable gloves so that his brother's fingerprints and DNA weren't on the device if it got found, but he hadn't considered the size of John's hands. The gloves split as he pulled them on.

After rolling the chair out from under his mum's desk, John found thin plastic file wallets to put over his hands instead of the gloves and stuck the bug on without a hitch.

Robin had also supplied a memory card with various bits of hacking software. But it seemed as if Sheriff Marjorie used her laptop, because the twin desks were clear apart from box files and charging cables.

Sherwood Castle security logged every time a security pass was used, so John needed to leave the office and tap back into the penthouse if the excuse that he'd popped in quickly to grab a printout was going to stand up.

But the detailed architect's model drew John's attention again as he took his printout. It had the gluey smell of something made recently, and he realised it was a version of Sherwood Castle very different to the one he was standing in.

The exterior fences were doubled up, with coils of barbed wire between them. The two side entrances were gone and the main entrance had a bunker-like gatehouse. Most dramatically, the castle's golf courses had been replaced with an exercise yard and long huts with corrugated metal roofs.

At the bottom of the board on which the model sat was a name plaque.

# Aitchison Correctional Corporation Sherwood Castle proposal

**Immigration and detention facility**
- 1500 maximum security in cells
(Category 2 male)
- 450 maximum security in cells
(Category 1 & 2 female)
- 4430 dormitory beds
(Category 3 & 4 male or female)

The implications of the model made John inhale so hard he practically swallowed his tongue. Sherwood Castle was tanking as a luxury resort, so his mum planned to turn it into a massive prison? His chest felt tight as he pulled out his phone and took several photographs of the model and the plaque.

As he leaned over the model to take a photo from behind, he noticed a cardboard box filled with brochures beneath the table on which the model stood. The front of the brochure bore the Aitchison Correctional Corporation logo.

John took the top copy and flicked through, seeing pages of detailed graphs, along with architects' plans, multicoloured tables and renderings of Sherwood Castle reimagined as a prison. Back on the first page, he skimmed the introductory paragraph:

**The facilities at Pelican Island prison are severely dated and the costs of maintaining an island prison are excessive.**

**A new state-of-the-art facility will be cost-effective and will increase inmate capacity by more than 30% ...**

As Little John continued to read, he noticed that King Corporation wasn't mentioned anywhere.

Besides being the elected Sheriff of Nottingham, his mum was a director of King Corporation. The company had a contract to run everything in Sherwood Forest and its crown logo was everywhere, from local destination signs to napkins in Sherwood Castle's breakfast buffet and on guard uniforms when he visited his dad in Pelican Island prison.

John had heard all the rumours about King Corporation refusing to fund Sheriff Marjorie's bid to run for president and firing her as a company director when her term as Sheriff ended. But the model and brochure showed that his mum had plans of her own, and he remembered what Pauline said the night before: *Sheriff Marjorie thinks six steps ahead of everyone else. And she's at her most dangerous when she's got her back to the wall*

There was a whole box of brochures, so John figured one wouldn't be missed. He stuffed the brochure inside his tracksuit top, but it bulged so he decided to roll it inside his battle map.

The lock in the office door clicked.

John gasped, snatched the map and rolled the brochure inside it as the beefy tweed-suited figure of Moshe Klein stepped into the office.

'Here he is,' Moshe said, sounding warm as he spoke to someone outside. 'We've been looking all over for you.'

# 17. SECOND CLASS CITIZENS

By noon the downpour had eased. Robin gave Lyla a break from navigation as Sherwood Designer Outlets came into view. Months of record-breaking rain had left the southern legs of the H-shaped mall and the surrounding car parks flooded. Robin kept the throttle on a low setting as he steered around a muddy embankment.

'Slightly left,' Lyla ordered, as she saw outlines of parking bays below the floodwater. 'There's a wall I've scraped a few times if you're not careful.'

Robin was cold and soggy, but flattered that Lyla trusted him with the helm for the tricky final metres of their journey.

With many supplies coming by boat, a temporary dock had been rigged in the mall parking lot. A dozen small boats bobbed in the chest-deep water and a narrow pier made from wooden delivery pallets linked it to dry land at the mall's main entrance.

'Turn, dummy!' Marion yelled as Robin came in at too steep an angle.

The idea was to approach crabwise and nudge the deflated car tyres hanging over the dock. Robin went in too steep, so the bow whacked the dock and the whole structure shuddered.

'My bad!' Robin apologised as Marion threw a rope to a woman on shore.

'I've seen worse,' Lyla told Robin happily, leaning across to show him how to shut the outboard motor off.

Robin gathered his backpack, bow and the bags of clothes Auntie Pauline had got him. As he stepped onto the pier, three older teens dived into the boat to begin unloading. A girl carrying sacks of rice almost bowled Robin into the water as he stopped to check out the Castle Guard boat he'd helped capture the day before.

'The family got lost,' the young woman told Robin. 'But they arrived before dark. They want to thank you guys for saving them, when you get a moment.'

Robin let a couple more people carrying cargo get by, then jogged down the wobbly pier to Sherwood Designer Outlets' main entrance. The water around the entrance was just puddles. Marion had reached dry land first and Robin wondered if she'd get upset again as she hugged her mum, Indio.

'Sorry I lost my phone,' Marion said sheepishly.

'Can't blame you this time,' Indio said. 'I'm glad you're safe. It sounded scary.'

'I'm fine,' Marion said. 'You know me, Mum.'

Robin wished Marion had been more open about her feelings. But before he knew it Indio was hugging him and asking how his family reunion had gone, while Marion was getting mugged by two of her brothers.

'I don't know anything about presents,' Marion teased, as three-year-old Finn tugged the back of her hoodie and seven-year-old Otto tried unzipping her backpack.

'We spoke to Aunt Lucy,' Otto shouted. 'She gave you presents for us.'

'Brats!' Marion complained, letting Otto pull her pack down her arms. 'Can't you wait two minutes?'

If you'd stepped through Designer Outlets' main entrance before summer, you would have entered the central bar of the H, and found a deserted atrium under a large glass dome. It got used as a security checkpoint on market day and you might have heard shouts and clattering skateboards from a rowdy pre-teen gang that used the upper floor food court.

But floods had brought thousands of desperate arrivals from the forest plains. While most moved north after a day or two's rest, several hundred of those unwilling or unable to do so had wound up stuck in this central area.

As Robin stepped inside his ears filled with voices, footsteps and screaming kids, but his nose took the main assault, breathing in an earthy mix of cooking, damp clothes and toilet facilities built for shoppers, not permanent residents.

Apart from puddles below leaks in the mall's fragile roof, things felt closer to normal as Robin followed Marion's mum past a security checkpoint into one of the mall's two northern spokes, then inside the abandoned sports store the Maid family called home.

Mall boss Will Scarlock was an idealist who said that newly arrived refugees should have the same rights as anyone else. But thefts, fights and turf battles had almost turned into a riot when the mall population exploded, so he'd reluctantly agreed to restrict flood victims to the central atrium and a sprawling campground on the dry northern car parks.

As Marion was about to turn off the main hallway into the sports store, she heard her name called from the roof through a broken skylight. Robin looked up and recognised Unai, a roofer and handyman who devoted most of his waking hours to preventing Designer Outlets from leaking, and increasingly from collapsing altogether.

'I know it's Sunday,' Unai told Marion from the rooftop. 'But I need some hands to fix the central skylights.'

Indio put a protective arm around her daughter. 'Marion's been through a lot, Unai. She needs to rest.'

But Marion pushed her mum away. She was tired, but it was the middle of the day. She'd never sleep with three mad brothers and baby Zack in the den, and she'd hate having nothing better to do than sit around reliving the night before.

'Honestly, I'd rather keep busy,' Marion yelled up to Unai.

'That's my girl!' Unai said, as Indio gave him a filthy look. 'And I need the famous idiot too.'

Robin didn't exactly hate Unai. The roofer was a decent guy who never stopped working, but he moaned about everything Robin did.

'The chore rota has me helping Sheila in the chicken sheds,' Robin answered. 'She's breeding extra birds so there are eggs for everyone.'

Unai smiled. 'I bumped into Sheila. She says you can be excused to work with me.'

Robin huffed and Marion smirked.

'Why do you want me?' Robin yelled up to Unai. 'Last time I helped, you hurled a paintbrush at me and said I was as useful as an inflatable dartboard.'

'You're small,' Unai said. 'And you climb like a monkey.'

Marion smiled and gave Robin a nudge. 'If Unai's asking for *your* help, he must really need it,' she whispered.

Robin had been looking forward to a chilled Sunday afternoon in his upstairs den but knew he should do the right thing. 'Fine,' he yelled up to Unai. 'But if you start moaning I'm gonna walk.'

# 18. WHEN DORKS COLLIDE

Little John tried to stay cool, but his cheeks burned and his entire body had erupted in sweat.

'What brought you down here?' Moshe asked.

'Printout,' John explained. 'I needed a big map for my History project.'

As John held the tube of paper up for Moshe to see, the brochure he'd hastily rolled inside made it start to unravel.

'Surprise!' Clare Gisborne said cheerfully, as she stepped into the office behind Moshe.

'Oh,' John said, baffled, as he tightened the rolled paper.

'Don't get *too* enthusiastic!' Clare said, rolling her eyes.

'Why are you here?' John said, trying to fake a smile.

'Asked the 'rents if I could take my brothers out for tacos,' Clare explained. 'But Mum said having them mucking about in the car would be a distraction. So I cruised on my own and got inspired by a sign pointing to Sherwood Castle . . .'

John interrupted. 'If you'd called I would have come down to reception and met you.'

Clare snorted. 'But then I wouldn't have underwhelmed you with my arrival.'

'I'm glad you're here,' John said defensively, as he gave her a peck on the cheek.

'There was no answer when the concierge called up to the penthouse,' Clare explained. 'So Mr Klein kindly helped me track you down.'

'Security passes get logged every time you go into a room,' Moshe explained. 'I could tell you'd entered this office.'

'I had no idea you could do that,' John lied. 'Thanks!'

He clutched his printout tightly and felt sick as he headed out of his mother's office.

'We can hang in my room,' he said as Moshe gave Clare an obedient nod and jogged to a waiting lift.

'Was I supposed to tip him?' Clare whispered as she followed John up the curved stairs to the penthouse.

John snorted. 'Moshe is my mum's top security guy. He's not short of a few quid.'

'He certainly looks fine in that suit,' Clare purred. 'Mmmmmm-hmm.'

John tutted as he tapped his security card to enter the penthouse. 'I thought you only had eyes for me.'

'I won't stick around long,' Clare said. 'I know you want to get your essay finished.'

'I'll take you over my History essay,' John said, as he led Clare to his room. 'You drove all this way.'

He fought the urge to snog Clare long enough to unfurl the map on his desk and slot the prison brochure in the drawer below.

'This massive bed is awesome!' Clare yelled, as she kicked off her trainers and jumped aboard. 'Can I destroy your pillows?'

The neat bedspread and Pia's symmetrical pillow arrangement flew in all directions as Clare did a back-flip on the bed.

'Get over here,' she said, clicking her fingers.

'Just making sure my work is saved,' John said.

'Not sure about that tracksuit,' Clare said as John clambered onto the bed.

'It's comfy,' John said. 'I wasn't expecting company. I can take it off if you like . . .'

Clare laughed as John took off his tracksuit top and twirled it around his head like a stripper.

'Happy seventeenth,' she said.

They kissed for a bit, but they'd only made the leap from mates to boyfriend and girlfriend when they started Year Twelve a few weeks earlier.

John hadn't had a girlfriend before and felt anxious, wondering if Clare expected something beyond kissing. Clare knew she liked John enough to miss him when he wasn't around, but she hadn't thought beyond the surprise and the birthday kiss and now she was on her boyfriend's bed with no adults around . . .

It was a relief to both of them when Clare's phone started ringing.

'It's the first time I've been out in the car on my own,' Clare told John, as she slid her phone out of her leggings. 'Ma is probably worried.'

As Clare sat on the edge of John's bed, telling her mum that she'd driven to her friend Karen's house, John remembered the brochure. With Clare staring out at the forest, he took the brochure from his desk drawer and locked himself in his bathroom.

He uploaded the photos he'd taken of the architect's model to a file sharing site, then rested the brochure on the toilet lid and knelt down to take photos of the cover, followed by each of the seven double-page spreads inside.

He was uploading the files and sending Robin a link to download them when Clare rapped gently on the door.

'Have you got another girl in there?'

'I was busting for a dump,' John said, sending the link to Robin and dropping the brochure in the drawer under his sink.

'How romantic!' Clare laughed, as John flushed the unused toilet.

'Sorry!'

'You know . . .' Clare began, backing up as John unlocked the bathroom door. 'I mean . . . I guess . . . I'm sending mixed signals. Turning up here and jumping on your bed. Then I get spooked and go all stiff when we're kissing. I really like you, but . . .'

'I really like you,' John replied, as his phone bleeped. 'It may have escaped your notice, but I'm not exactly Mr Suave myself . . .'

He glanced at the screen and saw that Robin had replied instantly with:

**That was FAST! Will download pics.**

Clare sat on the bed, pushed hair off her face and started laughing. 'We're such dorks . . .'

'We are,' John agreed.

Clare's laugh and the cute way she looked into her lap when she was embarrassed reminded him why he liked her so much.

'We could just hang out,' Clare suggested. 'It's called Sherwood Castle *Resort*. There must be something fun to do.'

John nodded. 'I know a good spot.'

# 19. DIRT, MOULD AND MOISTURE

Designer Outlets' main hallways had large oval skylights, and Marion, Robin and Unai stared up from a first-floor balcony at a particularly cracked and grotty example.

'Sealant around the glass has worn away,' Unai explained, his Armenian accent turned to a rasp by years of heavy smoking. 'Last week a pane dropped out and almost killed a kid on a tricycle.'

'I heard that,' Marion said. 'Pretty scary.'

'All these skylights are the failing,' Unai said, spreading his arms out to indicate the hallway. 'They're beyond repair.'

'If it's hopeless, can I go snooze?' Robin asked cheekily.

Unai gave Robin an extra-hard scowl as he lifted a roll of chunky nylon netting from his equipment cart.

'We'll stretch this under each skylight,' Unai explained. 'To catch if glass falls.'

'It's a long way up,' Marion said, as she studied the painted metal beams beneath the roof.

Robin had scared his mum by climbing on top of a garden shed before he could walk. He loved the mix of skill and danger in climbing and was already plotting his route: shuffling up a post from the first-floor balcony, then a leap onto the beam beneath the skylight and . . .

'OK,' he said happily as he wrapped his arms around a post.

'Stop!' Unai yelled. 'If you fall you'll bash your head in. First, we'll stretch netting between the balconies to catch you.'

'Seems like a waste of net,' Marion said. 'Robin has a thick skull and his brain is a tiny pea-like structure buried deep inside . . .'

Robin gave Marion the finger. He knew having a safety net was sensible, but for his thrill-seeking side, less danger meant less of a buzz.

As Unai, Marion and random people who realised help was needed stretched the safety netting between balconies on the mall's upper level, Robin received the message from his brother.

> **Found important stuff in Mum's office.**
> **Click link to download.**
> **Busy with Clare. Talk later.**

Robin was impressed that Little John had got inside his mum's office and found stuff so quickly. He didn't have time to look, so he bounced everything to Sam Scarlock in the rooftop command tent.

A small crowd gathered as Robin clambered easily up the pole to the roof, then hopped onto a cross-beam that spanned below the skylight.

The beam was barely wider than Robin's boot, and there were two problems. First, the beams supported large light fixtures, and while the bulbs inside burned out years ago they swung unpredictably when he straddled them. Second, birds lived under the roof. Robin wished he'd worn gloves, because there were droppings everywhere.

'Give us a wave, Robin!' some joker shouted as they snapped pictures from below.

Unai had worked out the netting procedure in advance. Once Robin was in position, Unai fed up a rectangular piece of netting hooked to the end of a barge-pole. Marion's job was to pre-cut lengths of scaffolders' strapping, so all Robin had to do was wrap each strap around a beam and snap a metal buckle to lock the net in place.

Robin was balanced beneath the third of five skylights that Unai said were in the worst shape when his phone rang.

'Hey,' mall boss Will Scarlock said. 'Can you join us in the command tent straight away?'

Robin looked down from the beam and laughed. 'Kinda busy . . .'

'The information Little John sent through is extraordinary,' Will continued. 'I've got people here analysing it. Unai's got a brain for mechanical things and his wife is here already, so ask him to come with you.'

Robin sighed. 'I'll be there as soon as I can.'

# 20. NICE GIRL, SHAME ABOUT THE POLITICS

'Where are we going?' Clare asked.

Little John led her by the hand as they crossed thick carpet between roulette wheels and craps tables. The whoops and bleeps of slot machines rose up the escalators from the main floor below, but this upper level of Sherwood Castle's casino had been shut down while business was slow.

'It's not golf, is it?' Clare asked. 'I know I said I was up for anything, but I do draw the line at golf.'

'Ta-da!' Little John said as they reached a locked metal shutter between an American-style diner and casino cashier counter, both closed.

'A shutter,' Clare said, giving it a gentle kick. 'You sure know how to treat a lady!'

The shutter had a door cut in one side, and a tap of Little John's access card opened it up. He ducked through the opening and felt along a side wall, seeking an electrical panel.

'Are you planning to murder me?' Clare asked as her eyes adjusted to darkness.

John found the panel and pulled a big handle. Multicoloured lights flashed across the ceiling, along with the electronic chimes and flashing lights of more than sixty machines. Mini-bowling, test your strength, air hockey, coin drops, pinball, wheel of fortune . . .

'My little brothers would love this,' Clare said, as John stepped behind a service counter and took two VIP lanyards from a pegboard.

'You tap the disc and any machine is free,' John explained, hanging a lanyard around his neck. 'They built this by the casino to keep the little snots occupied while Mummy and Daddy gamble the rent money.'

'My own private arcade,' Clare said, clearly impressed, as she approached a punch bag machine. 'Wanna see who's toughest?'

John laughed. 'You've whacked me enough times to know that answer already.'

'I bet I could high-kick it,' Clare said, as she tapped her badge to start a game.

John found a crane grab machine nearby. 'These things never work,' he told Clare. 'But I found the way to get a prize.'

After going on tiptoes, John forced a lock and swung out a clear plastic panel that gave him access to a mountain of furry squirrels and hedgehogs.

'AAAARGH!' Clare screamed, as she displayed her kickboxing skills and blasted the punch bag with her sneaker.

'Maximum score,' an electronic voice announced, as the display on the front read 999. 'You are a total beast!'

'I'm a beast,' Clare roared, flexing her biceps. 'Get over here and show me what you've got, John Boy!'

'So you like the arcade?' John said, pleased that he'd done something Clare liked as he lobbed a furry squirrel at her.

He took a shot at the punch bag, scoring 365 as the machine told him to keep practising.

'I'll use my fist this time,' Clare said, dropping into a boxer's stance as the punch bag came down. 'Take aim and imagine it's a refugee's face . . .'

'Great score!' the machine announced, as the red LEDs flashed up 635.

'Did you say a *refugee's* face?' John asked, outraged.

'Yeah,' Clare said, cracking a mean grin. 'Just because I've stopped worshipping the ground my daddy walks on and I'm dating Robin Hood's brother, doesn't mean I've turned into some migrant-loving pansy.'

John shook his head and threw another squirrel at Clare. 'You'll be eighteen by election day. You can vote for my mum, like all the other psychos who hate migrants, benefit seekers, homeless . . .'

'Can and will,' Clare said proudly. 'I don't get why you take your dad's side. Your mum is a superstar. She was born with *nothing*. She founded Captain Cash when she was our age and became a millionaire by twenty. Then she ran for Sheriff as a massive underdog and wiped the floor with everyone.'

'I'll see if I can get you discount membership to her fan club,' John joked.

'I'd love to meet her.'

'I told her we're friendly,' John said. 'But she doesn't know we're dating.'

'Think she'll mind?' Clare asked.

John shrugged. 'Not as much as your dad. Seeing as he whipped me and Robin shot him in the nuts.'

'My plan is not to tell Dad I'm seeing you until our golden wedding anniversary,' Clare joked. 'And can we *please* stop talking about parents and politics? We came down here to have fun.'

'Mini-bowling?' John suggested. 'Or the zombie shooter game?'

# 21. AROUND THE BIG TABLE

Designer Outlets had two-hour queues for hot showers, so Robin tried to imagine he was back in the fancy student crib in Locksley as he stood around the back of Unai's equipment shed and let Marion blast him with water out of a hose.

'You can look now!' Robin told Marion, as he wrapped a towel around his waist and ran into Unai's shed, to be greeted by an eye-watering smell from leaky cans of roof sealant.

Marion had fetched clean clothes for Robin. She didn't complain about having to pick up his dirty clothes and stay behind to put all the equipment away, because he'd done all the hard work fixing the nets.

'See you back at the den,' Robin said, taking his phone and some other junk out of his dirty trousers.

He shivered as he hurried across the mall's puddled roof to Will Scarlock's command tent.

The spacious ex-military tent sat directly beneath a rickety wooden watchtower, designed to give Designer

Outlets' security teams a clear view of anything approaching through the car parks.

'Young Mr Hood,' Will Scarlock said fondly as the teen stepped into the tent. 'You look knackered!'

Will was in his fifties and always capped his bald head with a garish bandana. His sons, nineteen-year-old Sam and eighteen-year-old Neo, sat around the tent's giant planning table, along with Unai and his wife.

'You scrubbed up OK,' Unai said.

Robin sniffed his fingers. 'I still smell bird poop. I need to get a brush under my nails . . .'

'My wife Jeanne,' Unai said, introducing Robin to a slim, serious-faced Frenchwoman with bright yellow nail varnish. 'Jeanne is a mechanical engineer. So she's the brains of the family and I'm the good looks.'

Jeanne shook her head, like she'd heard Unai's joke too many times before.

Robin stepped up to the planning table and saw lots of maps and papers spread out, including pages from the brochure. But it was a photo of the model of Sherwood Castle converted into a prison that caught his eye.

'The info my brother sent was useful?'

'Superb,' Will Scarlock said.

'I only expected him to plant the listening device,' Robin said. 'I thought it would take days just to get snippets of useful conversation from Sheriff Marjorie.'

'Sometimes you get lucky,' Neo Scarlock said, nudging a seat towards Robin. 'Take the weight off. You look tired.'

'Does Marjorie want to turn Sherwood Castle into a prison?' Robin asked, as he rolled up to the big table.

'That's what it looks like,' Will said. 'We've been going through maps and tables in an architect's proposal document your brother sent over. After some extra digging online, we're beginning to understand what Marjorie has been up to lately.'

'We looked up Aitchison Correctional Corporation,' Neo said. 'They run prisons in twenty countries, making them King Corporation's biggest rival in the private prison industry.'

Robin thought for a second, then nodded. 'Everyone says King Corporation are going to fire Marjorie's arse. But my Auntie Pauline has known Marjorie all her life and says she's at her most dangerous when her back is to the wall.'

'Couldn't have put it better myself,' Will agreed.

Jeanne took up the story in a thick French accent. 'The really interesting part of the proposal brochure is small print of the final pages. Converting Sherwood Castle into a prison will be expensive. Perhaps more expensive than building a new prison from the ground up.'

'Why do it then?' Robin asked.

'There is a cost breakdown in the brochure,' Jeanne explained. 'The money for converting Sherwood Castle Resort into Sherwood Correctional Facility is mostly paid by the Emergency Flood Administration.'

Robin looked baffled as Will took over the explanation.

'The Emergency Flood Administration – EFA – is a government body that hands out money after severe floods,' Will explained. 'It was meant to provide help for flood victims to rebuild damaged homes, or restart businesses. But the money is paid to local government, so Sheriff Marjorie gets to decide how any EFA money for Sherwood Forest is spent.'

'Like, spending it all on converting Sherwood Castle into a prison, and leaving people whose houses got flattened with nothing,' Sam Scarlock added.

'OK,' Robin said, trying to get all this straight in his head. 'Sherwood Castle Resort has no customers and is about to go bust. Marjorie buys the castle on the cheap with her new partners, then uses emergency flood money to convert it into a prison?'

'Pretty much,' Will said, as the others nodded. 'But that's not the whole picture. And you're here because we need you to ask Little John for more help.'

'He'll be at boarding school all week,' Robin said.

Jeanne slid a map of Sherwood Forest and the Macondo River in front of Robin and continued.

'Sherwood Forest has flooding every year,' she began. 'To get money from the EFA, flood damage must be *extreme and unusual*. For the last couple of months I have been studying the releases of water from the four dams upriver, trying to understand what is happening.'

'The ones that cause the surges?' Robin asked.

'*Exactement!*' Jeannie said enthusiastically. 'My questions is this: why is water released from the dams quickly and violently? And the river splits into several channels as it passes through the forest, so why is water released in the same place, over and over?'

'I guess if the water is released more violently it causes big surges and more damage,' Robin said. 'And if it blasts through the same part of the forest over and over, the damage becomes *extreme and unusual.*'

'And Marjorie gets her EFA money,' Will said, giving Robin a pat on the back. 'Smart kid, isn't he?'

Jeanne continued as Robin smiled at Will's compliment. 'There is also a third reason to release floodwater in certain channels only: it protects Sherwood Castle from flooding.'

'Wouldn't the resort go broke faster if it flooded?' Robin asked. 'Wouldn't that be better for Sheriff Marjorie?'

'Sherwood Castle has three basement levels. A flood would greatly increase the time and cost of converting it into a prison,' Jeanne explained. 'The project needs a high profit margin to fund Marjorie's presidential campaign.'

Robin nodded. 'And if Marjorie becomes president, instead of her private army of a few hundred Castle Guards, she'll be Commander in Chief of the real army.'

'Along with her policies to place all undocumented people in internment camps,' Will said. 'Slash pensions and welfare, abolish the minimum wage, create a *business-*

*friendly environment* by abolishing safety standards and environmental rules, and bring in charges for doctor visits and hospital treatment.'

'Basically, making the country worse for everyone who isn't one of Sheriff Marjorie's rich chums,' Neo added, to polish off his dad's rant.

'But Marjorie can't win an election without tens of millions of pounds for organisation and advertising,' Will said. 'And now we we've found out how she plans to make the money, we're going to do our utmost to stop her.'

'Like how?' Robin asked.

'I've only made preliminary calculations,' Jeanne said. 'But my idea is that the next time water is violently released from a dam upstream, it ends up in the basement of Sherwood Castle.'

# 22. BOUNCY BALLS FOR THIRTY TOKENS

Like a kid who opens an expensive toy and plays with the bubble wrap, Little John and Clare Gisborne had an arcade with half a million quid's worth of games but wound up chasing each other, lobbing ten-pence bouncy rubber balls at each other from behind the ticket redemption counter.

'Death to the running dog capitalist pig!' Clare yelled as she blasted ball after ball at John.

He was pinned behind an air hockey table, but he gathered what Clare threw and when he had a dozen balls he sprang up and started chucking them back.

'Oww! Not the face!' Clare yelled, as she retreated.

'You hit me in the face twenty times!'

John was a big lump, so people were always surprised by his speed. Clare dived and crawled between two arcade cabinets. John was too broad for the gap, so he ran around as Clare scooted about, gathering loose balls off the carpet.

As John came around the end of a row of cabinets, Clare was in his way, reaching for a ball. She pushed up, giving John a mighty shoulder barge into a two-player arcade cabinet where the players sat on fake motorbikes.

'Whoa!' John yelled.

As Clare laughed and threw bouncy balls, John slid over one of the motorbikes and got stuck between them, head on the carpet and feet waving in the air.

'I'm stuck!' John groaned, as Clare ran out of balls and started picking up ones she'd already lobbed.

As John waggled his legs, Clare thought it was the best thing ever and wanted to film him on her phone, but she was laughing so hard she could hardly stand up.

John grabbed the rear wheel of a fake motorbike, tightened his stomach and launched a mighty two-footed back-kick. It set him free, but one heel pounded the game's display and the screen changed from a shot of racing bikes to flickering white with a web of cracks in one corner.

'You busted it!' Clare said, still laughing wildly. 'You knob!'

John didn't see until he'd crawled out of the gap. 'My mum will go nuts,' he gasped.

'Only if she finds out,' Clare said.

John yanked the machine's plug out of a floor socket, because a dead screen would draw less attention. 'I'm knackered,' he gasped, as he used another arcade cabinet to pull himself to his feet.

Clare held her stomach because she'd laughed until it ached.

'It wasn't *that* funny,' John complained.

'It so was. Your legs up in the air, all the blood rushing to your head!'

'Glad you find me so entertaining.' John tutted. 'I need a drink, I'm wiped.'

'This has been the most fun I've had in ages,' Clare said, as she kicked a bouncy ball under an arcade cabinet.

John nodded. 'Sometimes you need to act like an eight-year-old.'

'I saw a Coke machine by the front desk.'

'It's empty,' John replied. 'But I have unlimited expenses, so we could go down to the café by reception.'

Clare stopped walking and grabbed John for a kiss. She backed off after a few seconds, but John thought it was the best kiss they'd had, because they'd made their own little world, not thinking about parents, rebels, essays, listening devices, school . . .

They were back at the arcade door and John was about to shut the power off when a motor whirred and the metal shutter began rising. The light beneath felt like real life coming back, and this feeling grew as they saw the polished shoes of two tweed-suited Sherwood Resort security guards.

John wondered if trashing the motorbike racer had set off an alarm. 'Can I help, ladies?' he said, as it occurred to him that they probably thought breathless seventeen-year-olds stepping out of an abandoned arcade had been up to something far naughtier than throwing bouncy balls.

The guard on the left tapped to indicate her radio. 'Moshe Klein called,' she explained. 'Your mother's helicopter is due in a few minutes. She wants to speak to you the moment she arrives.'

John felt wary as he pointed at Clare. 'I'm hanging with my friend.'

Clare shrugged and gave John a sad look. 'I should probably get home. I'm newly qualified, so I can't drive after dark.'

John was gutted that his afternoon with Clare was over. 'See you at school tomorrow, I guess.'

Clare sighed. 'Weekends always go so fast.'

John felt OK as he watched Clare go down the escalator to the ground floor. But he sensed something was off when he walked towards the lift and the guards moved in step behind him.

'I live here,' John said irritably. 'I know where I'm going.'

'We're sorry, sir. Mr Klein told us to keep you in sight until you reached the penthouse.'

The other guard added, 'He also asked us to take your mobile telephone.'

John felt wobbly. He should have deleted the photos of the architect's model, but Clare's arrival had thrown him off.

'It's my private phone,' John said firmly. 'I'm not an employee.'

The guards glanced at each other. Since John was Sheriff Marjorie's son and weighed more than the pair of them, they settled for the fact he was heading to the penthouse lift.

# 23. HATE IS A STRONG WORD

The penthouse lounge had a stone fireplace big enough to park a car inside, long leather sofas and a fancy glass desk. The kind of desk where nobody ever worked and the only things on it were granite sculpture thingies that cost a heap of money.

Except today, Moshe Klein sat behind the desk and a proposal brochure from Aitchison Correctional rested on the glass.

'You don't learn German at Barnsdale,' Moshe said, sounding pleased with himself as John entered with his guards.

'German?' John said, as Moshe waved the guards out.

'I worked in Israeli intelligence,' Moshe explained, as sweat from chasing around the arcade turned to chills down John's back. 'They train agents to look for tiny details. Like someone who doesn't speak German printing a campaign map written in German.'

'Clare arrived,' John said. 'I haven't looked. I'll have to print a different one.'

As John spoke, the windows were buffeted by a helicopter approaching the landing pad two floors down. Moshe tapped the brochure as if to say, *Why bother lying?*

John felt shaky and was still thirsty from running around. Moshe's eyes tracked him as he walked to a cocktail bar at the back of the lounge and took a bottle of water from a glass-doored fridge.

He didn't want Moshe to see his hands tremble as he scooped ice into a crystal tumbler and poured the water on top. His mouth was a desert and it seemed to take a hundred years for Sheriff Marjorie to walk up from the helipad.

It had been six months since John found out he was the product of a drunken encounter between two old school pals: Marjorie Kovacevic and Ardagh Hood. The first time he met Sheriff Marjorie was weird: discovering that a politician he'd been taught to hate was not only his mother but she had sent her guards into the forest to save his life.

But if that scene had been awkward, seeing his mum come into the lounge, dressed smart for a TV interview but with her make-up smudged by tears, was worse. And her hands trembled as much as his own.

'You must *really* hate me,' Marjorie said, wounded.

She didn't look at John, going straight for the bar and a generous tumbler of whisky.

'I never expected prizes for motherhood, but I thought we were doing OK,' she continued. 'I looked forward to flying home after a tiring day and eating with my son.'

'I don't hate you,' John said, staring down at his Nikes.

Moshe was a statue as Marjorie smacked her empty tumbler on the bar and stormed up to John. 'Are you just going to stand there like a dope?'

'Mum . . .' John began, but couldn't make his tangled thoughts into words.

'I leave you on your own for a few hours. The first thing you do is sneak down to my office, steal a confidential document and send it to your brother and his rebel friends.'

'It's not like that,' John said.

'Then what is it like?' Marjorie spat. 'Tell me. After all I've done for you. What goes on in your head that makes you betray me the instant I walk out the door?'

John didn't answer and Moshe spoke for the first time in ages.

'When the Animal Freedom Militia destroyed our summer trophy hunt, Robin and his pals used *your* security pass to escape through a side entrance,' Moshe said.

John tutted. 'I left my card in the dining room when they started throwing smoke bombs. One of the AFM dudes must have picked it up.'

Marjorie shook her head slowly. 'Everything that's gone wrong for me these past months is because of that raid.'

'I swear, I knew *nothing* about the raid until you did,' John said truthfully.

'I've only issued four access cards with full clearance,' Moshe said. 'Myself, my deputy, your mother and you. Isn't it a remarkable coincidence that your card ended up in Robin's hands?'

John groaned. 'We went through all this three months ago.'

'And I believed you,' Marjorie said. 'But now I'm not sure.'

John glanced at his mum, glanced behind at Moshe and decided to try a teenage strop. 'I've got an essay to write,' John shouted dramatically. 'Think what you like. I'm going to my room to work.'

He only got two steps before Marjorie blocked his path.

'If you were anyone but my son, I'd have Moshe and a couple of guards work you over and dump you in the forest,' Marjorie roared.

'That's why I'm *so* proud having you for a mother,' John yelled back. 'Robin told me about the guards they found in the forest, setting bear traps that can rip a kid's leg off.'

'Robin the beloved boy hero!' Marjorie mocked, before erupting in a false laugh. 'A brat who runs wild and shoots officers with a deadly weapon? He'll spend his life in jail for terrorism. And the way you're going, so will you.'

'I guess you and your mate Gisborne can frame Robin like my dad,' John spat.

'Sherwood Forest is all around,' Marjorie said, spreading her arms out wide. 'If you want to go, go. Find your rebel chums. Live in mud, drink river water. Eat beans from a can instead of room service steak, and sleep on a rubber mat instead of your cashmere-topped mattress.'

John was lost for words, because his mum had read him perfectly.

Marjorie sensed victory and laughed. 'I sign off the fancy food on your room service tab, the limited-drop tracksuits and two-hundred-quid rugby boots that go on my credit card. And don't forget your new girlfriend, Clare. See if she fancies you when you crap in a hole and haven't changed clothes for a month.'

John was surprised his mum knew about Clare. Bringing her into the calculation almost made him tearful, but John resolved not to wilt under his mother's barrage.

'I don't hate you, Mum,' he spat. 'But I do hate all the things you stand for.'

John expected another blast and was surprised to see anger drop off his mum's face.

'Finally, something honest,' Marjorie said, before giving a dry laugh. 'But you live under my roof. If I can't trust you, what am I supposed to do?'

'I don't know,' John admitted.

'Things will have to change dramatically. Moshe made a list of suggestions.'

John turned and scowled as Moshe read a list on his phone.

'No online access, except through a single device supplied and monitored by me,' Moshe began. 'No trips outside of school, unless you are accompanied by your mother or a member of my security team. You will be issued with a new security pass that only gives access to this penthouse. All visits to your father will be cancelled and you must not contact Robin or any other rebels.

'Other privileges such as shopping trips and seeing Clare outside of school will only happen if you display excellent behaviour at all times. If you break any rules, your next stop will be the Iwo Jima Boys Military Academy. You've probably not heard of it, but they've straightened out lads a lot tougher than you.'

'Is he in charge?' John asked resentfully, as he gave Marjorie his best pleading eyes. 'Come on, Mum. Please!'

Marjorie shook her head and wiped a tear from her eye. 'You betrayed me. What do you expect?'

'I'll write a behaviour contract for the boy to sign,' Moshe said.

'I'm speaking to the boss, not her monkey slave,' John snarled, trying not to cry. 'Mum, please at least let me keep visiting my dad.'

'I need your phone and PIN,' Moshe said.

'No,' John said.

Moshe stood up from behind the desk.

'Give Moshe the phone,' Marjorie ordered. 'This is not a negotiation.'

Moshe went eyeball to eyeball with John. 'You may be taller and heavier than me, but you'll be sorry if you don't give me that phone.'

'I'm not scared of you,' John hissed, then made another attempt to storm out.

Moshe expertly swept John's feet away and shoved him in the back so he sprawled face-first into a big leather couch. Then Moshe dug his knee in the small of John's back and twisted his thumb into an agonising lock.

'PIN,' Moshe demanded, as his free hand extracted Little John's phone.

'Mum, make him stop,' John begged.

Marjorie saw a tear streak down her son's face but stayed tough. 'You've nobody to blame but yourself.'

'PIN,' Moshe repeated, forcing back John's wrist to double the pain.

'Four, five, nine, one,' John cried.

As Moshe let go, John whimpered and clutched his twisted hand to his chest.

'Behave for your mother,' Moshe roared thuggishly as he wagged his finger in John's face. Then he looked at Marjorie. 'Don't forget we've got cells in the basement if he causes more trouble.'

# 24. THE BEST-LAID PLANS

Jeanne's idea to flood Sherwood Castle would be the most complex operation the rebels had ever attempted. In the west, they needed to take control of flood gates for the four dams along the Macondo River. In the east, they had to disable flood defences at Sherwood Castle.

Robin stayed in the command tent through Sunday evening, debating options with Jeanne, Unai and several members of the Scarlock family.

Buildings can't be built or altered without permission and since the Sherwood planning department kept its archives online, Jeanne easily downloaded detailed plans of Sherwood Castle Resort and hundreds of planning documents, including ones relating to flood prevention.

'Any large structure built in the Macondo River Basin must have flood defences,' the engineer explained as she leaned over the big table with Robin and the others gathered around. 'The best option is robust physical defences that rely on gravity and soil absorption. Well-designed barriers, drainage channels, porous concrete and so forth. But building natural drainage is time-consuming and expensive.'

Will Scarlock laughed. 'And Sheriff Marjorie loves a fast profit.'

'She certainly did with Sherwood Castle Resort,' Jeanne agreed. 'You can save money building expensive groundworks by installing pumps. The pumps suck up water and spit it out a safe distance downstream. Systems like this are quite effective, if the pumps work.'

Unai cut in. 'This blasted mall was built with pumps. If we had natural drainage and higher foundations, the southern legs wouldn't be neck deep in water right now.'

Robin smiled. 'So to pull this off, we have to kill the pumps at Sherwood Castle?'

Jeanne nodded. 'Any sudden surge of water may cause minor damage, but working pumps would deal with most of it.'

'We have sympathisers with jobs inside the castle,' Will Scarlock told Robin. 'But based on the castle plans Jeanne downloaded, the pump room is in a secure area at the rear of the casino. The only person with security clearance is your brother.'

Robin nodded. 'Thing is, it's Sunday night and Little John's at boarding school Monday to Friday.'

'That's why we really wanted you here earlier,' Will said, as he glanced at a big clock nailed to one of the tent's support poles. 'It's almost ten, but your brother might be able to get down there tonight.'

'Not to sabotage the pumps,' Jeanne added. 'First we need photographs of the equipment, and any documentation he can steal. Modern pump systems are technically sophisticated, with sensors and remote monitoring.'

Robin's eyebrows shot up. 'Remote? As in online?'

Jeanne smiled. 'They might be hackable, yes.'

'Sweet.' Robin grinned.

'Flood pumps are too important to fail,' Jeanne explained. 'Large pump systems are programmed to run daily tests and automatically contact a service technician if there's a fault.'

'Online fault detection,' Robin purred. 'Probably allows full remote system access if I can . . .'

Brothers Sam and Neo Scarlock saw Robin deep in thought and laughed.

'Look at our cybergeek go,' Neo joked.

'Love a good hacking challenge,' Robin admitted.

Unai snorted. 'What about the old-fashioned way? Drop a few sticks of explosive and blast the pumps to hell.'

Will Scarlock shook his head. 'What if we set off a bomb and someone gets killed?'

'Sheriff Marjorie will call us terrorists and claim someone was killed or burned, even if we're careful,' Sam added.

Jeanne sensed the conversation getting ahead of itself and rapped on the table. 'Let's focus, guys!' she said firmly. 'Whether we hack pumps or blow them up, we need information first. So Robin, can you please speak to your brother and see if he can get in there tonight?'

'John's probably still awake,' Robin said, as he picked his phone off the table, opened a shielding app to hide his location from anyone trying to track him, and pressed the call icon. 'But he already risked his neck for us once today. He's not gonna be happy.'

Robin rolled his chair back to the edge of the tent where it was quieter, but he had to leave a voicemail. Then he sent Little John a text message to be sure.

Will sighed. 'If we can't get Little John, I can call a few of our friends who work at the castle. See if they know anyone with access.'

'Someone in the maintenance department,' Jeanne suggested.

Sam Scarlock tutted. 'Trouble is, the more people who know what we're up to, the more chance someone tips Marjorie's people off.'

Robin's phone pinged and he smiled as a bubble popped up with a message from Little John.

**Can't talk. Watching movie with Mum. What do you need?**

'Got hold of my brother!' Robin told everyone cheerfully.

But Little John was slumped on his bed in the penthouse feeling sorry for himself, and his phone was three floors down in the hairy hands of Moshe Klein.

# 25. THE NIGHT DOESN'T END

Little John's night was all stress and no sleep. He tried figuring out if he loved or hated his mum and realised the answer was a bit of both. And was he a bad person himself, for living in luxury with the money she made?

Part of Little John wanted to run off into the forest and fight injustice, part of him liked the idea that he could soon be the president's son. Cruising in the presidential jet and living in the Freedom Palace. But the biggest part of John wanted to ignore all the complex stuff and be a regular seventeen-year-old. Go to school, play rugby, write boring essays and hang out with Clare . . .

With his bedcovers in knots and zero chance of sleep, John stood by his window watching the moonlit clouds and swaying treetops.

With no easy answers, he decided the only thing was to take one day at a time. He'd be at school the next five days and things might be less tense with his mum when he got back on Friday. If it stayed weird, maybe he'd ask to become a full-time boarder . . .

At first light, John reached for the bedside telephone to order breakfast. But Moshe had taken it away, along with his laptop and console. He'd even blocked Wi-Fi on the televisions in case John found a messaging app.

John thought about waking his mum and asking how he was supposed to order breakfast with no phone, but the thought of facing her again made him queasy, so he headed for the bar in the lounge, wearing just boxers.

He considered orange juice, but Monday was always a long day and since he hadn't slept he pulled the tab on a Lemon Scorpion energy drink.

He was heading back to his room to gather his schoolbooks and put on uniform when Moshe came in the main door. The security chief had an apartment three floors down and wore clingy shorts and sneakers, like he was about to hit the gym.

'Good morning, young man,' Moshe said, with a cheerful arrogance that made John loathe him more.

'What's good about it?' John grunted, then glugged his can of Scorpion.

Marjorie knew Moshe had arrived and came out of her bedroom, wearing giant furry slippers and scratching her armpit.

'Is that junk your breakfast?' Marjorie asked John, acting the concerned mother.

'Got no phone to order food,' he answered sourly.

'We need another talk,' Moshe told John.

'I have to get ready for school.'

'I've been catching up with your little brother,' Moshe said, as he pulled John's phone from the pocket in his T-shirt. 'Robin sent a copy of *my* work rota, because apparently you wanted to know when I wasn't going to be around.'

'How could Robin get that?' Marjorie asked.

'StayNet,' Moshe revealed. 'John's rebel pals have hacked our entire admin system.'

Marjorie looked shocked and glowered at John. 'Seriously?'

'We thought something was off,' Moshe explained. 'Staff rotas changing. Hotel bookings refused when we have empty rooms, cleaning staff getting huge overtime payments. The IT department spent days trying to figure it out.' Moshe turned back to John. 'And you've been contacting Robin through a messaging system hidden in a hacked podcast app.'

John looked shocked and Moshe laughed.

'Don't be surprised,' Moshe said. 'I have contacts whose understanding of cybersecurity is more sophisticated than your thirteen-year-old brother's.'

'Where does this betrayal end?' Marjorie groaned, planting her hands on her hips and staring at John.

'And what do you know about the pump room?' Moshe asked.

For once, John was genuinely clueless.

'I'll be late for school if I don't get a move on.'

Marjorie shook her head. 'At school you can borrow a phone to alert Robin.'

'I have to go to school,' John said dopily.

'I'll let Barnsdale know you've come down with a nasty cold,' Marjorie said. 'You can return in a few days when we've unpicked this mess.'

'StayNet wasn't me,' John said, sounding desperate. 'I knew Robin could access the system, but I had nothing to do with the hack.'

'Pumps,' Moshe said again, as he scrolled on John's phone and read a message from Robin in a mocking kid accent. '*Sorry to ask when you already put your neck out today. But we need you to get in the pump room for pics and info ASAP.*'

John shrugged. 'I didn't know we had a pump room.'

'Why are the rebels interested in pumps?' Marjorie asked Moshe.

'I guess Robin wants the ability to switch the pumps off the next time there's a flood,' Moshe said confidently. 'I've already disabled remote access to the pump room and put two guards on the door.'

'Better safe than sorry,' Marjorie agreed, then shot a sly look at John before adding, 'Let's discuss operational details in private.'

Moshe nodded and went back to proving how clever he was to Little John. 'I read your messages to Robin over several months,' Moshe said. 'He mentioned how grand it was to see you on your birthday and speak to your father in his cell.'

Marjorie glowered. 'You said you slept over with a school friend.'

Moshe smiled. 'We could get in touch with the warden at Pelican Island. Evidence of a phone in Ardagh's cell will wreck his chances of early release.'

John backed up to the hallway wall and imagined hurling one of his mum's expensive vases at one of her even more expensive paintings. But he'd just end up with Moshe pinning him to the floor. He had to toe the line, or pretend to.

'Please don't drop my dad in it,' John said meekly. 'I'll cooperate.'

'Get dressed,' Marjorie told John, as she swiped the half-drunk Scorpion can out of his hand. 'I'll order a proper breakfast. I have meetings in Nottingham. You'll stay here under guard today. If Moshe needs answers and you don't fancy military school, you'd better be straight with him.'

John hesitated, making Marjorie angrier.

'I play golf with the warden at Pelican Island,' Marjorie warned.

John tutted and looked at Moshe. 'If he's stolen my messages, he knows everything already.'

'Get dressed,' Marjorie repeated.

But as John walked back to his room, all he could think about was finding a way to let Robin know Moshe was tricking him.

# 26. LOVELY PAIR OF BUNS

Robin was up past midnight, researching ways to hack pumps and sending messages to what he thought was his brother.

First thing Monday he wanted to sleep in, but Marion woke early and was clattering around on the other side of their den.

'It's ten past six,' Robin complained, peeking out of one gluey eye. 'What are you doing?'

'I can tell the time,' Marion said, as she stood with one foot on a chair, lacing her boot. 'I've taken six of your carbon core arrows.'

Robin sat up. Marion's laptop was open on the dining table and the screen ran a brightly coloured 3D animation of the Macondo River Basin, complete with dams and flowing water.

'Where are you going?' Robin asked.

'Go back to bed,' Marion said happily. 'You need all the beauty sleep you can get.'

But Robin was too geeky to ignore the simulation on Marion's laptop and was already crossing the floor wrapped in his duvet. The laptop ran fluid-modelling software and Robin saw there were loads of slider controls on screen with names like 'Darley Dale Slipway 2' and 'Predicted Rainfall Zone 4'.

Robin realised that by resetting the model, then changing settings and releasing water from different dams or opening different overflow tunnels, you could simulate how different combinations would cause flooding in different parts of the forest.

'Jeanne made this after I went to bed?' Robin asked, as Marion loaded a backpack with binoculars, a knife and packed lunches. 'She really knows her stuff.'

Marion nodded. 'Jeanne sent it to me so I could get an idea how the system works. But she says we need more data because a lot of the settings are guesswork.'

'How long have you been up?' Robin asked, then repeated, 'Where are you going?'

'I'm in the Deadly Viper Recon Squad,' Marion said proudly, zipping up a thick vest with lots of equipment pockets. 'My alarm went an hour ago. I ate breakfast, made sandwiches for four, got my gear ready. And before you ask, yes, I did empty the water buckets under the leaky bit of our roof.'

'This simulation is so cool,' Robin said, as he turned one of the rainfall sliders up to maximum and watched Locksley vanish in a biblical flood.

'Me, Jeanne, Lyra and her big sister Azeem are taking a boat up to Old Road. Then by road to scout the four dams and the Water Authority Control Centre.'

Robin looked ticked off. 'Nobody mentioned this trip to me.'

'Oh no!' Marion mocked. 'Do you mean Robin Hood *isn't* the centre of the universe?'

Robin was too sleepy to bite back, and was glad that Marion had something to keep her mind busy after she'd felt bad the day before.

'Can't even remember falling asleep,' Robin said. 'Little John sent some info about the pumps last night, from an operations directory his mum keeps in the penthouse. He said he'll try going to the pump room this morning before school.'

'Sounds like a plan,' Marion said, as she snapped her laptop shut and put it on a high shelf out of little brother Finn's reach.

Robin noticed an extra foil-wrapped sandwich next to the laptop. 'Is that going spare?'

Marion nodded. 'Made it for you when I did the lunches. I knew you had to be up early too.'

'Do I?' Robin said, mystified.

'Chicken Sheila,' Marion said, shaking her head. 'You helped Unai yesterday, but Sheila wants you at the chicken sheds before school to make up for it.'

'Great,' Robin said, as he unravelled the foil-wrapped sandwich and sniffed bacon.

'Good job I reminded you. She would have been down here jabbing you awake with her walking stick,' Marion smirked.

'Forecast says we'll catch the tail of Storm Verity later,' Marion explained. 'So Unai might need help later too.'

'I'm so over this weather,' Robin moaned, looking up at the dripping mall roof above his den. 'There hasn't been a dry day in two months.'

'They say it's record-breaking,' Marion said, as she pulled her pack on and grabbed her bow. 'But Verity might be doing us a favour.'

'How?'

'Big storm makes for a big flood.'

'True, dat,' Robin said. 'I still think Will and Jeanne are crazy, trying to pull off a scheme this complex in a day or two.'

'Gotta run. Azeem and the others will be waiting downstairs.'

'Don't get killed,' Robin joked, enjoying a bite of his breakfast sandwich as Marion jogged out of the den and slid down an escalator to the first floor.

Robin thought about getting back into bed, but worried he'd fall back to sleep. So after checking his phone to ensure Little John hadn't sent any more information through, he put on his grubby work clothes and headed to the rooftop chicken sheds.

Drizzle whipped into Robin's face as he stepped onto Designer Outlets' roof. The sun barely poked over the treetops, but there were already more than thirty people queuing for showers.

Robin bought two hot teas and fresh-baked buns from a stand that was just opening up. When he looked over the edge of the roof he could see driving wind blast through the refugee encampment in the northern car parks and at least one tent threatening lift-off.

'Morning,' Robin said. His hands were full, so he hooked his boot around the wooden door on the newer of Sheila's two chicken sheds.

The heat, noise and ammonia smell of a crowded coop could be overpowering, but Robin was used to it. The wild-haired Chicken Sheila was already at work, limping amidst hundreds of birds and tossing handfuls of dry feed. She glanced at her watch and seemed disappointed.

'Can't yell, cos I'm early today,' Robin teased. 'And I'm such a nice boy, I bought you a cuppa and a warm bun.'

Sheila grunted. 'Suppose you'll sit stuffing your face for half an hour.'

Once Robin realised that Sheila moaned about everything, he'd learned to take it in his stride and was secretly fond of her.

'Lovely buns when they're fresh,' Sheila admitted, as she took the paper bag with the bun Robin had bought her. 'But no messing about! Go in the old shed, check the incubator. The lamps keep popping.'

'It's the damp,' Robin said, as Sheila took her tea. 'I pulled the incubator out the other day. The roof is leaking and the electrics behind are wringing wet.'

'Did you put my three sugars in?' Sheila asked, then after Robin nodded to confirm, 'All my joints hurt with this damp. I'm barely sleeping.'

'It's too much work now there's two sheds,' Robin said. 'There are loads of bored refugees who'd help out for a few cartons of eggs.'

Sheila shook her head, as if letting someone else near her beloved chickens was the worst idea ever. Robin knew better than to argue and set off for the old chicken shed as he chewed the last mouthful of his bun.

'Hello, girls!' Robin told the chickens as he stepped in.

Sheila kept her chickens in relative luxury, with plenty of space, clean cages, perches to jump off and things to peck at. The flock charged towards the wire fence, knowing Robin would feed them, then clucked impatiently as he dealt with the incubator.

The cabinet was the size of a fridge, with egg-filled drawers. Each level had lamps and a heating control. Three birds had hatched overnight in the middle tray. Robin flicked bits of shell off chirping yellow bundles and released them into a tabletop pen with a wire lid to stop rats getting at them.

Total mayhem erupted as Robin gave the flock a giant bag of green stuff picked from the forest. While the birds scoffed, Robin entered the cage with a plastic tub and walked about gathering eggs.

There were twenty in the tub when his phone started vibrating. After wiping his mucky hands on his work trousers, he pulled out the phone and saw a message from Little John's account.

> **Files dropped. Hope it's what you need.**
> **Gotta get to school now.**

Robin was keen to see what had been uncovered and opened the online vault he used to share encrypted files.

Sherwood Designer Outlets' Wi-Fi was sluggish because so many people were always online, but he opened several photos of a pump room, along with close-ups of control panels and ID plates showing device models and serial numbers on various pieces of equipment, including the switch that linked the system to the internet.

'Nice job, Little John,' Robin said to himself.

Jeanne and Will would want to see what he had straight away, so he forwarded the link with another short message.

> **Mission accomplished — see attached**
> **files :-)**

# 27. DEADLY VIPER RECON SQUAD

The Deadly Viper Recon Squad had four members. Sherwood Outlets' security chief Azeem and her younger sister Lyla were the muscle, mechanical engineer Jeanne was the brains, and Marion was small, stealthy, and could take someone out silently with her bow.

The dams at Bolsover and Stanton were twins on opposite sides of the Macondo, brimming with floodwater and a couple of staff in high-vis overalls doing maintenance. After Jeanne had satisfied herself taking photos and laser measurements, a half-hour drive took them to the next dam at Youlgreave.

This larger dam was the only one built with a road crossing and a viewing deck at midpoint. Since the weather was foul and most tourists were scared to enter Sherwood, the four women had the vandalised deck to themselves.

As they lunched on bacon sandwiches, the dam put on a show with three huge rain gates opening and water blasting down a concrete slipway to the river.

'Is that a surge?' Marion asked.

'Nowhere near,' Jeanne said, as she leaned over a railing and pointed down the outer face of the dam. 'They're releasing rainwater to stop it flooding over the top. But if you look down at the base of the dam, there are two much bigger flood gates.'

Marion leaned over the rusty railing, looked down a hundred metres of sheer concrete, and saw them through the haze of rain.

'Fully opened, they can release about a hundred times more water than the rain gates,' Jeanne explained. 'An Olympic-sized swimming pool in every second.'

She pointed down to where the dam's concrete slipway met the river. 'Those gates are only meant to be operated in an emergency, such as rain gates jamming, or structural damage in an earthquake. But look at the far side of the river, and you can see how everything has been churned up.'

Marion nodded as she looked at a sea of mud, and several wooden buildings ripped apart by blasting water.

'The head of the Water Authority says that opening emergency gates and causing surges is an operational necessity caused by freak rainfall,' Jeanne explained. 'But he refuses to answer technical questions on why water can't be released more gradually, and his boss is Sheriff Marjorie, who's keen to flush out Forest People and get money from the Emergency Flood Administration.'

Azeem had been keeping lookout, and glanced about warily as she stepped up to the rusty railing. 'Someone in Water Authority overalls is checking us out with binoculars,' she warned. 'Probably harmless, but why stick around longer than we have to?'

Before they got back in their battered pickup truck, Marion couldn't resist balling her sandwich crusts in their foil wrapping and dropping them a hundred metres down the face of the dam.

'Litterbug,' Lyla complained, before doing the same with hers.

The largest dam and the Water Authority's Control Centre were at Darley Dale, another ten kilometres west. While Bolsover, Stanton and Youlgreave dams blocked tributaries that fed into the Macondo River, Darley Dale dammed the Macondo River itself. A kilometre of concrete spanned a flooded valley, and the few boats that went this far upriver had to divert through a series of locks.

The only road to the top of the dam was a three-kilometre track behind a locked gate, so Azeem parked the truck behind an abandoned backpackers' hostel while her sister used bolt cutters to make a hole through the fence.

The quartet kept low as they hiked rocky ground, sometimes so steep that they held on to bushes to pull themselves up. Jeanne was in her sixties and struggled to the point where Lyla held her arm and Azeem took her equipment.

When Darley Dale opened almost a century earlier, it had been the longest dam in the world, and a source of national pride. As they neared the columned entrance of the Control Centre, Marion was surprised to see rows of overgrown parking spots and direction signs for a shuttered museum and café.

The whole squad were amazed when they reached the highest point of the hill and looked down at the vast dam and a manmade lake stretching back several kilometres.

'Storm Verity,' Jeanne said, as she glanced the other way at fast moving clouds circling over the forest. 'I'd say it's over Locksley right now. Hopefully, we'll get back before it reaches Designer Outlets.'

Lyla looked through binoculars and studied the Control Centre. Two cars were parked out front, along with a large utility truck in the livery of the Macondo Water Authority.

'Two cars means two people,' Lyla suggested. 'Unless someone car-shares.'

'Doesn't seem many for such a huge site,' Marion noted.

'All four dams are controlled from in there,' Jeanne said, still catching her breath after the hike. 'There are more people working in the hydro-electric power plants, but those are at the base of the dam almost two kilometres from here.'

Lyla kept looking through her binoculars. 'It's a flat roof. Someone could climb up. There's probably an access hatch.'

Azeem scanned the Control Centre roof with her own binoculars and didn't sound keen. 'There's a lot of rusty barbed wire up there,' she noted.

'Cameras?' Marion asked.

'Can't see any,' Azeem said.

'Peeling paint, cracked windows,' Lyla added. 'I'd say zero pounds have been invested around here in the last few decades.'

Azeem sounded more positive after she spotted a frosted glass window that had been propped open. 'That has to be the toilet.'

Marion scanned through her binoculars until she saw the window. 'I could get through that gap.'

'I've got the thermal imaging camera,' Lyla said, as she lowered her binoculars. 'I can hold it up to each window so we know where the workers are before you go in.'

Jeanne looked at Marion as Lyla prepared the thermal camera. 'Do you understand what I need from inside?'

Marion nodded. 'You found photos of the control room online. But we need precise info on how the system works, so we're looking for manuals, maps, diagrams.'

'Exactly,' Jeanne agreed. 'As far as I know, the control system hasn't been updated since the four dams were built. So most things will be on paper.'

'If they catch me, I'll act like I'm a robber after wallets and car keys,' Marion said.

'Thermal cam powered up,' Lyla said. 'Azeem, come with me and give close protection. Marion, keep your bow handy and prepare to shoot anyone who—'

'Isn't it beautiful up here?' a cheery voice yelled from behind, making the four women jump. 'Even in this weather.'

# 28. THE DAM BUFF

The Deadly Viper Recon Squad were startled, and embarrassed – they'd been so focused on how to get inside the Control Centre, they'd allowed someone to sneak up behind.

Marion notched an arrow as she spun around. But while her imagination saw gun-toting killers, reality was a jowly bloke in his eighties. He wore a long purple waterproof with matching hat and spotless white trainers that meant he was no forest dweller.

'You shouldn't be up here,' the man said. 'Didn't you see the signs?'

Marion realised the rain and wind that had allowed the old man to sneak up had also prevented him from hearing them plotting to break into the Control Centre.

'We didn't realise,' Jeanne said, thickening her French accent and hoping to play a tourist who didn't know better.

'Not that you'll come to much harm,' the man said, laughing so hard his belly shook. 'Had eight guards on patrol across this site in my day. But when King Corp took over they said they could do it all with drones. But do you know a funny thing about drones?'

'They can't fly in heavy rain,' Marion suggested.

'Clever girl!' the man said, giving Marion a huge smile and wagging his finger. 'And these days, it's always raining.'

'You worked here?' Azeem asked.

'Retired now,' the man answered, nodding. 'I hope you don't find me rude, but I saw you pass the café and thought I'd step out and say hello. The name is Randall.'

'The café?' Jeanne said. 'I thought everything was closed.'

'Tourist centre shut down donkey's years ago,' Randall said. 'I'm a volunteer with the Macondo Historical Society. We do guided dam tours Monday and Saturday. Had two booked in for this afternoon but they didn't show. No surprise with a storm coming, but they might have let me know and saved me a trip.'

'We can book a tour?' Azeem asked, as she gawped at her sister.

Randall nodded as the rain pelted his hat. 'I made the tour website.'

'I teach in the engineering department at Nottingham University,' Jeanne said, now she'd had time to think up a story. 'This is my granddaughter Claude. Mari and Beck are students from my course. Maybe I am crazy in this weather, but I thought coming up here might inspire them.'

'Well, isn't that lovely?' Randall said warmly. 'I worked here, man and boy.'

'So you know all about this dam?' Marion asked.

'There's no piece of gear in Darley Dam I've not stripped and repaired at some point,' Randall said proudly. 'I was going over to Kev and Lakshman in the control room for a coffee. I don't have time for the full tour, but you're welcome to pop in if you fancy a quick nose.'

'That would be incredible!' Jeanne said. 'Nobody will mind?'

Randall laughed. 'Not if you leave your mucky boots at the door.'

Marion thought it mad that a building that controlled four dams with reservoirs large enough to flood and destroy huge areas of land had so little security. And after all their discussions on how to get in, Randall walked through the unlocked main door yelling, 'Only me, boys!'

Marion unlaced her boots in the lobby, then looked up at a high ceiling with elaborate plasterwork and a sculpted brass light fixture with most of its bulbs blown. There were cracks and stains from lack of maintenance, but no expense had been spared when the Control Centre was built.

The impression of faded glory grew as Randall led them through to the windowless control room. There was a metal viewing gantry along the back for visitors. Up front the control console resembled a church organ, lined with hundreds of switches, stops, knobs and gauges, most with the labels rubbed away from decades of use.

*Nothing for Robin to hack here,* Marion thought.

'Quite beautiful,' Jeanne said, as she inhaled the smell of switch oil and dusty electrics. 'It must have looked spectacular when it was new.'

Randall agreed enthusiastically as he introduced her to Kev and Lakshman. They both wore workman's boots, Macondo Water Authority sweatshirts, and the glazed expressions of twenty-something men whose job involved staring at gauges and ticking hourly checklists.

Kev and Lakshman seemed to regard Randall as something between a joke and an irritant. They barely nodded when the old man offered to make them coffee, but the pair perked up when they sighted Azeem and Lyla.

'Which button do I press to drown everyone?' Lyla asked.

Lakshman laughed harder than Lyla's dark humour deserved and Kev started blatantly hitting on Azeem, rattling on about some friend who was a DJ who ran an amazing underground venue in Nottingham, and if she gave him her number he'd get her a VIP pass even though it was sold out until Christmas . . .

As Azeem and Lyla worked on the Water Authority employees, Jeanne went into a side room to help Randall make coffee, and used the opportunity to ask detailed questions that he was delighted to answer.

This left Marion redundant. But she was wiped after the hike, so she found a chair, rested her damp socks on the warm rungs of a radiator and wished she hadn't lost her phone, because it would have helped kill the time.

# 29. BATTERY BY BABY

After eating an early, rowdy dinner in the Maid family den with Marion's little brothers, Robin headed up the escalator to the den he shared with Marion.

He'd posted on his favourite dark web hacker site earlier on, asking if anyone had experience hacking pump systems. Now he sat on his bed, listening to Storm Verity doing her worst as he read replies that were mostly spam, or dodgy people trying to sell him half a million hacked passwords.

Amidst the spam were thoughtful replies suggesting that Robin's options were to infect the programmable logic controllers inside the pumps with a Stuxnet virus, or sneakily capture login details used by the maintenance company when they accessed the pumps remotely.

Robin decided hacking the pumps was possible, but not without access to Sherwood Castle's pump room, and not if they were serious about pulling the operation off within days.

He felt defeated as he prepared to tell Will Scarlock that, unless they gave him more time, they'd have to go with Unai's suggestion and blow the pumps up.

Wind and lightning had been blasting the mall for over an hour. As Robin left his den he heard a weird splash, like someone dumping a paddling pool full of water. It came from the stock room at the back of the sports store, and he doubled back for his torch before checking it out.

More water splashed down as Robin passed the battered targets that he and Marion used for archery practice. A gust whistled through gaps in the building's cladding and the flat roof groaned under stress as he opened the stock room door.

Robin shone his torch down rows of empty metal shelves and saw that waves were running along the insulation panels below the roof and spilling into the shaft of the store's stock lift. There was clearly a big leak nearby, though the lift shaft exited into an external cargo bay, so at least the water was draining outside.

Marion was walking up the escalator as Robin headed back to their den. She'd said a quick hello when she got back from Darley Dale an hour earlier, but she'd gone downstairs to wash and eat so this was their first proper chance to catch up.

Her hair was damp from a wash, she wore an adult's towelling robe that almost touched the floor, and she had her five-month-old brother Zack in her arms.

'You smell like coconut,' Robin noted. 'How was Darley Dale?'

'We got lucky,' Marion said brightly, as Zack blew a raspberry. 'Bumped into this old-timer who runs tours. Jeanne got more information than she dared hope, and he even drove us back to our truck!'

'Wish I'd had as much success hacking the pumps.' Robin sighed. 'I'm heading up to the command tent to give Will the bad news.'

'Prepare to get wet on the roof,' Marion warned. 'Verity is a brute.'

To prove her point, another blast of wind sent another groan through the roof.

'There's a big hole somewhere nearby,' Robin said, as another splash hit the bottom of the lift shaft. 'We'll have to find it tomorrow in daylight.'

'Did you hear about my dad?' Marion asked.

Robin looked concerned. 'He OK?'

'The Brigands camp got engulfed by a mudslide. No serious injuries, but they had to leave bikes and most of their stuff behind.'

'Where are they heading?' Robin asked.

Marion shrugged. 'Will said they can shelter here if they want.'

Robin looked uncomfortable. 'The Brigands are a riot, but I can't see them repairing solar panels or joining Will's shower-cleaning rota . . .'

'It'll end in tears,' Marion agreed. 'If your trip to see Will can wait two seconds, would you hold this little guy while I finish getting dressed?'

'Sure,' Robin said.

'He's tired,' Marion said, as she passed Zack over. 'Matt and Otto are having their usual show-off about going to bed, so Mum asked me to take him out of the way.'

'Are you a tired boy?' Robin whispered, bouncing Zack gently.

'Just need trackies, socks and sweatshirt,' Marion said. She scrambled into the den. 'Don't put him down or he'll go bananas.'

Robin eyed the baby warily. 'Zack's gonna be good for Robin, aren't you?'

Marion's little brothers Finn, Otto and Matt often played on the escalators or in the area outside Robin's den. Although it was gloomy, Zack spotted a wooden cart that the boys pulled each other around in.

'GAAAA,' Zack said, lunging at the cart and catching the bridge of Robin's nose with the top of his head.

Robin gasped with pain and rebalanced. 'You're not riding now, it's bedtime,' he said, trying his most soothing voice and turning so Zack couldn't see the cart.

Zack didn't fall for the move and squealed.

'What did you do?' Marion yelled accusingly from inside the den.

'Nothing,' Robin protested. 'Can I come in? Are you decent?'

Marion was tying the waistband on the battered tracksuit bottoms she often wore to bed as Robin stepped back into their den. As Robin hoped, the change of scene and sight of Marion kept Zack's mind off the cart.

'Is that Marion?' Robin asked Zack as he rocked him. 'Is that your nasty big sister who smells like farts and pee?'

Marion silently mouthed a very rude word as she took Zack back. 'Thanks for holding him,' she said, then sounded alarmed. 'You're bleeding, dude!'

'Eh?' Robin said.

'Top lip.'

Robin brushed his finger across his face and smeared blood. 'Nosebleed!' he said, tilting his head back. 'Used to get them all the time when I was little. Zack just bumped me with his head.'

'Did you beat Robin up?' Marion asked Zack. 'Aren't you a clever boy!'

Robin glanced about, looking for tissues, but the box on the dining table only had one left.

'Mum has boxes of 'em,' Marion said, as Robin stuffed the tissue up his bloody nostril. 'Go get some.'

'Yeah,' Robin agreed, tasting blood in the back of his throat.

Marion was torn between feeling sorry for Robin and laughing her arse off as he hurried out of the den. He was about to leap the last three steps of the escalator when the roof groaned again, but this time it was louder than before and turned into a rumble, followed by a floor-shaking crash.

'What was that?' Marion blurted, as she ran out of the upstairs den.

Down below, Marion's mums Indio and Karma, along with Matt, Finn and Otto, had all run out of their family den and stared up to make sure they still had a roof over their heads. People were sprinting along the main hallway, and further off were the desperate screams of people who'd been badly hurt.

# 30. TORCH BEAMS AND DUST

'I'll see if they need help!' Robin yelled.

He ducked under the sports store's metal shutter and almost got blatted by a man running the other way. After dark you'd normally look down the hallway towards the main entrance and see flickering battery lamps and bustle from the refugees inside the main entrance, but now the air hung heavy with dust and the view was blocked by a shadowy tangle of debris.

'It must have affected Dr Gladys's clinic,' Karma said desperately, then shouted at Otto and Finn, who'd followed her out in their nightclothes. 'Back, you two, don't breathe in that muck.'

As Zack wailed and people down by the atrium pleaded for help, Robin watched juddering torchlight beams scan wreckage and people scrambling to pull out bodies trapped under the debris.

'There's plenty of people down there,' Marion said as she handed Zack off and tugged on Robin's hoodie. 'But Unai might need us on the roof.'

'Lift on three, two, one!' someone shouted down by the debris.

And another. 'Stop pulling – her fingers are trapped!'

Robin's nose hadn't stopped bleeding, and he spluttered blood and dust as he bolted after Marion to a set of spiral stairs in the centre of the mall corridor.

'You two be careful!' Indio screamed.

An emergency floodlight burst to life as Marion and Robin ran. The usual route along the mall's upper hallway was blocked by debris. As they clambered over, they saw that a forty-metre section of roof over the mall had crashed onto the refugee camp in the central lobby. Even more alarmingly, the large glass dome covering the food court had lost all the support on one side.

Beyond the debris was the high-end clothing store that served as the mall's medical centre. Nobody inside had been injured, but dust-caked patients and scarce equipment were being dragged out into the mall because the rain was pouring in.

'This is so messed-up,' Marion said, close to tears as they reached a balcony overlooking the central mall and realised that the steps up to the roof had collapsed.

Down at ground level, some of the flood refugees gathered their belongings and piled into the storm-swept northern parking lots, while others formed rescue teams, using whatever tools they could find to make holes in the collapsed roof and pull out people trapped beneath.

Robin looked at the dangling handrail of the collapsed rooftop steps and gave it a tug to see if it would hold his weight.

'If that comes down, it'll flatten you,' Marion warned.

'It's the only way up to the roof from this side of the mall,' Robin said, as drips pouring off the hole pelted his hair.

Marion could climb better than most, but she didn't fancy going hand over hand up a dangling metal stair rail, then along a slippery beam to an intact section of roof.

'Looks like they need help getting patients and equipment out of the clinic,' Robin said.

'Maybe we should both—'

But before Marion could finish her sentence with 'help in the clinic', Robin gripped the rail and pulled himself up.

Marion wondered if Robin's lack of fear when climbing would get him killed some day as she watched his rain-lashed silhouette reach the roofline, then his hoodie and tracksuit bottoms fill with wind as he crossed a metal beam to safety.

'All good,' Robin yelled down, as he patted his pocket and felt for the torch he'd used to check out the lift shaft.

As Marion clambered back across the rubble to help inside the clinic, Robin spotted Unai, Will Scarlock and a few others staring into a rectangular hole. It was twenty metres wide and forty long, with the half-supported glass dome teetering over one end.

'Anything I can do?' Robin asked as he approached.

Unai was in the middle of an explanation, and didn't pause. '. . . Most of the bolts holding up the roof beams are corroded. When one beam fails, the weight on the next beam doubles, so that fails too. Then the next, and next, and next until it reaches the main concrete truss.'

'A cascade,' Will Scarlock said.

Unai nodded. 'Luckily, I saw the beam starting to buckle and told everyone to evacuate the area below. Most left before the collapse, but some were reluctant to go out in the storm.'

'Could more sections fail?' Neo Scarlock asked as another violent gust whipped across the roof, making the dangling dome whistle and one of its glass panes crash down into the lobby.

'The rest of the roof has smaller spans and more supporting walls than the atrium,' Unai said.

Robin was relieved to see that the falling glass hadn't hit any of the rescuers.

'We always knew this was the weakest part of the roof,' Will added. 'We've always kept it clear.'

'This type of roof is meant to be stripped and replaced every twenty-five years,' Unai added. 'This one is past forty.'

Will Scarlock had spent years transforming Sherwood Designer Outlets from dodgy bandit hideout to a well-organised rebel community. He looked devastated. 'We've lost the southern legs to flooding, now there's no roof over the centre . . .'

Robin felt useless, rubbing his bloody nose on his hood as he looked down at the rescue teams.

Azeem's voice came solemnly through the radio strapped to Will's belt. 'They found two more. That's five confirmed dead and eight seriously hurt, over.'

Will smudged away a tear as he answered. 'Roger that, Azeem. Any sense of how many are missing?'

'The rescuers have cut or dragged away most of the fallen roof sections now, so we're praying that's it,' Azeem said.

Unai made a *give me* gesture and took Will's radio. 'Once you're certain, clear the area,' he told Azeem. 'That dome weighs eighty tonnes. If it comes down, it could take the other side of the atrium roof with it.'

'Nobody wants to hang around down here,' Azeem agreed. 'Some panels also smashed into our temporary dock. I've sent people out to secure the boats.'

'Damn,' Will Scarlock shouted, stamping his foot and pounding a fist into his palm.

'We'll sort it, Dad,' Neo said. 'It's been a rough few months, but we always get through.'

At the same time Robin felt his phone vibrate in his pocket. The blasting rain made it hard to hear when he answered. 'Who is this?'

Robin missed the reply and turned his back to the wind.

'Who?'

'Jeanne,' she repeated. 'Can you hear?'

'Barely,' Robin said, putting a hand over his other ear as another blast of wind made the glass dome shudder.

'We've got a *big* problem,' Jeanne said. 'The pictures Little John sent contained a virus. I'm locked out of my laptop. When I went to update my Macondo River simulation, it crashed and rebooted to a purple screen.'

'You're kidding!' Robin gasped. 'Have you got security software?'

'Sure,' Jeanne said. 'But when I click the repair button, the antivirus crashes and opens to some weird webpage full of Chinese ads. It wouldn't shut down with the power button and it was getting hot, so I've taken the battery out.'

After the rain, the roof and the nosebleed, the idea that Little John had sent Robin infected computer files felt overwhelming.

'Are you still there?' Jeanne asked.

'Thinking,' Robin said, after a pause. 'Where are you?'

'In the command tent.'

Robin glanced across the soggy rooftop and realised the hole was in his way. But there was still plenty of roof left for him to cut around the edge.

'I'll be with you in one minute,' he said.

# 31. THE CURLY MOUSTACHE

Little John had spent all day alone in the penthouse, with all phones and web-enabled devices removed by Moshe and a burly Castle Guard outside with instructions not to let him leave.

He tried doing some reading for his essay, but focusing on Napoleon seemed impossible when his whole life was upside down. With no phone, John went to the lift lobby to tell the guard what he wanted for lunch, but barely managed to eat.

John nosed around his mum's bedroom out of boredom and a hope he'd find some forgotten device. The only interesting things were a key card in a bedside drawer and an old photo album with pictures of a teenaged Marjorie, Ardagh Hood and Guy Gisborne mucking around on a Geography field trip.

He browsed through some of her fancy books of weird art and well-thumbed business tomes with titles like *Get Everything You Deserve* and *The Twelve Keys to the Billionaire Club.*

There was also a printout of an Iwo Jima Military Academy brochure, with scribbled notes from a conversation with the Dean of Admissions making it clear that his mum wasn't bluffing. The Academy looked like a tough joint, with lots of pictures of boys climbing nets and marching around in big shiny hats.

Decisions always stressed Little John, and he liked the idea of being in a place where everything from the length of your hair to the time you went to bed was decided for you. But the thought of being sent thousands of kilometres from Clare, Robin and his dad was unbearable.

As John watched Storm Verity through the penthouse lounge's huge windows, he thought about the amazing afternoon messing around with Clare in the arcade. It felt like years ago and he wondered what she'd been up to all day at school.

He kept the lights off and curtains open as Sherwood took a blasting. The forest was a depressing reminder that Moshe was probably using his phone to lure Robin and the rebels into a trap. But he still couldn't think of a decent plan to warn his brother, and when worry turned to a stomach-churning angst he went for the bar.

To spite his mum – whose helicopter couldn't fly until the storm passed – he took the fanciest-looking bottle from an illuminated bar shelf. He broke the seal, took a slug and decided that fifty-year-old Glen Haddock whisky was revolting.

But it wasn't bad when he added ice and Rage Cola. After two tumblers and with all digital forms of entertainment blocked, he noticed his mum's record player and put on the cheesiest pop record he could find.

After three tumblers, he had the brilliant idea to get a big marker pen and either write *Robin Hood Lives* or draw a big curly moustache on one of her paintings.

But trashing art worth millions guaranteed him a one-way ticket to military school, so he chickened out and wound up on a big sofa with the world softened by the booze and the vinyl at the end of the side making a crackly noise thirty-three times per minute.

He was feeling sorry for himself and thinking how nice it would be to cuddle up with Clare when genius struck.

John sprang drunkenly to his feet. He began by turning over the record and putting the volume up so loud it made the cones of his mother's expensive loudspeakers wobble like jelly. Then he took a stack of black cocktail napkins from the bar and the spare toilet roll from his bedroom, and stumbled into the guest toilet off the penthouse's main hallway.

After lifting the toilet lid, John dropped in the napkins, unravelled the entire loo roll on top and packed it all down using the toilet brush. When he hit flush there was nowhere for the water to go, and it quickly filled the bowl and began spilling across the floor.

John hadn't realised that it would spray violently enough to soak his trackie bottoms, so he stood further back when he flushed again and doubled the size of the flood.

As John stepped into the hall, the water was trickling nicely along the marble hallway tiles. He opened the door into the elevator lobby and saw a guard squatting on the floor looking bored off his head.

'Can I help you?' the guard asked, polite and a little nervous as he stood up. 'More food?'

John opened the big door enough for the guard to see his wet tracksuit and the water trickling into the hallway.

'Toilet's broken,' John said. 'Tried to fix it but the flush is jammed.'

The guard was clearly no genius and just gawped at the puddle.

'Call maintenance now,' John said, hoping he sounded less drunk than he felt. 'Last time this happened, the tiles came up and my mum went bananas.'

The idea of Sheriff Marjorie going bananas perked the guard up. He unclipped the radio on his belt and looked at the channel selection knob.

'Do you know what channel is maintenance?' he asked.

John acted like he was super worried. 'These marble tiles cost thousands . . . Mum fired a guy on the spot last time this happened.'

'Right, right,' the guard said, fumbling with the channel selector before speaking into it. 'This is fourteen-sixty with a maintenance request from the Sheriff's penthouse. Water coming out of a toilet. Can we get someone up here fast?'

# 32. DON'T MESS WITH LITHIUM BATTERIES . . .

Jeanne was alone in the command tent as the wind rippled the heavy fabric and the two-storey wooden watchtower above creaked eerily.

'What happened to your face?' she gasped as Robin ran in.

'Just a nosebleed,' he answered, breathless and low-pitched because the bleeding had mostly stopped, but one nostril had clogged with blood. 'It always looks more dramatic than it is.'

Jeanne's elderly laptop was on the big planning desk, along with a bunch of plans and dam drawings spread around.

'Careful, it's hot,' Jeanne said, as Robin looked over her dead laptop.

'I've heard about this,' Robin said. 'Most computers have fans to keep cool. If a virus can override the thermal sensor, it gets hotter until your system fries.'

Robin opened the glass door of the server cabinet at the back of the tent, which controlled the mall's internet, and linked it to the satellite dish up the watchtower.

'I assume you were using our Wi-Fi?' Robin asked, as he slid out a keyboard shelf and logged into the main server. 'What time did you open the pictures?'

'About two hours ago,' Jeanne said. 'When I got back from Darley Dale.'

Robin saw a red security warning box on the server screen. Since hundreds of people used the mall's Wi-Fi, there were always security warnings. Robin opened the security panel and scrolled down a list to an entry at 17:37:

```
Unidentified threat — May contain signature
elements of or similar to Tambourine S34
virus.
WARNING: This virus can override thermal
protection and cause physical damage to
infected systems.
```

Robin smiled with relief.

'Our web server detected your virus, which is good because it could have burned out a very expensive server and infected anyone using mall Wi-Fi.'

'But I had antivirus on my laptop,' Jeanne said.

'Even the best virus software can't detect every threat. You're lucky you had an old laptop where you could take the battery out.'

'Do you think your brother knew he was sending infected files?' Jeanne asked. 'Did you send them to anyone other than me and Will?'

'I trust my brother,' Robin said, but before he could finish this thought, he realised he'd looked at the pictures on his own laptop several hours ago . . .

It was his beautiful titanium gaming laptop and the most expensive thing he owned. But it didn't have a removable battery, and he often switched his security software off because it blocked most hacking tools and many of the dark web sites he visited.

'Are you OK?' Jeanne asked, as blood drained out of Robin's face.

'My baby!' Robin blurted as he sprinted out of the tent.

The rain had dropped off as he raced back across the roof. He slid down the broken stair rail, scrambled over rubble, ran along the hallway, down the spiral stairs, around startled patients and soggy equipment that had been dragged from the clinic, under the metal shutter of the sports store, took two steps at a time up the escalator and crashed breathlessly through the door of his den.

It was the fastest Robin had ever run. He'd bashed his knee landing on the debris, and dried blood from his nosebleed made him want to cough, but he ignored his body as he approached the laptop on his bedside table, thinking, *Please be cold, please be cold, please be cold* . . .

But he felt heat from a few centimetres away, and when he reached underneath to pick it up it was too hot to touch.

'Damn!' Robin shouted, glancing about, wondering what to do.

There was a dirty T-shirt on the bed, and he wound it around his hand before grabbing the laptop again and putting it upside down on the dining table. He flipped on a lamp and saw that not only was the machine whirring and hot, but the case bulged where heat had made the battery inside expand.

Robin knew that lithium batteries explode if they overheat. He'd even watched one destroy a police drone in mid-air a few months earlier. The best option was to move the laptop to a safe outdoor spot and let it blow, but Robin had used a heap of his cash-machine robbery money to buy the laptop so he slid his hacking toolkit off a shelf.

He steadied the laptop with the T-shirt and undid two tiny screws to release a sliding expansion panel. He unclipped the memory module, knowing that the machine – and the virus – couldn't run without it.

Robin was pleased to see the blue power light on the side of the case die, but loosening the case had also made more space for the battery to expand. This movement broke down barriers between volatile chemicals inside the battery, which created gas, which made the battery expand more, causing more damage, and more gas, until . . .

There was a sharp pop, then a high-pitched squeal of escaping gas. A white spark shot across the den as Robin booted the door open and flung his beloved laptop. It clattered onto the empty sports store floor outside the den and skidded further away, bowling Finn's trike out of the way then shooting up towards the roof, propelled by a white jet of burning lithium.

Robin shielded his eyes as his laptop exploded into shards of hot metal and plastic. He was scared that something else would catch fire, but the environment was damp from the leaky roof so things fizzled or steamed. Apart from the laptop itself, the only damage was three melted action figures and a shard of toughened glass embedded in an archery target.

'What happened?' Marion's ten-year-old brother Matt asked as he charged up the escalator.

Robin stared at the ceiling, shaking his head. 'That was an expensive lesson in why I need to turn my antivirus back on after playing with hacking tools.'

Matt was a noisy show-off kid. Robin was surprised that he didn't start charging around picking up bits of laptop and yelling *that was amazeballs* or something.

'Is Marion up here?' Matt asked, as he got close enough for Robin to see he'd been crying.

'I think she's still helping at the clinic. What's the matter?'

'It's all explosion dust,' Matt lied, rubbing one eye. 'Have you heard about Jasprit?'

'I don't think I know any Jasprit,' Robin said.

'You rescued her family on the river,' Matt said, then sobbed. 'Mum Indio said be nice to her when she arrived, so I showed her around. She was wicked at football and they just found her under the roof all crushed up.'

Robin struggled to take it in. 'Dead?'

'Yeah,' Matt said, as he completely broke down.

'Oh, mate,' Robin said, tearing up and pulling Matt into a hug. 'That's terrible.'

# 33. LONG RUBBER GLOVE

Little John's plan kicked off in a burst of drunken exuberance, but his confidence drained as he waited for the maintenance department.

He could hear his heartbeat as the penthouse bell chimed. It might be a suspicious Moshe, it might be a burly Marjorie-fanatic maintenance man. So he was relieved to see Laura, a redhead in her late twenties dressed in blue dungarees and holding a big tool bag.

'You again,' John said brightly.

'Me again,' Laura said, flicking one eyebrow as she eyed the streak of water across the lobby's white marble.

John didn't know Laura well, but she'd been in the penthouse before, once when the electric curtains in the lounge jammed and once on a routine stop to replace air conditioner filters. He'd even had a quick conversation about her twin sons and how her ex did one of Ardagh Hood's computer courses at Locksley Learning Centre.

'I guess I put too much paper down,' John said, as he shut the door on the security guard.

Laura's tool bag touched down with a metallic rattle as she opened the door of the guest toilet.

'What is this?' she gasped suspiciously as she looked into the toilet. 'That must be an entire bog roll.'

John took a breath and hesitated, feeling like his old self – the one who needed Robin to tell him if he needed a raincoat. He could forget the whole thing and let Laura clear the blockage and go, or . . .

'I need your help,' John gasped, as Laura kicked a little trash can towards the toilet and pulled an elbow-length rubber glove out of her bag.

'I'm here to help,' Laura said, clearly not relishing the idea of sticking her arm in the toilet.

She realised that John was drunk and his huge frame looming in the doorway was intimidating.

'I don't mean the toilet,' John said. 'I need a favour. Can I borrow your phone? I have to message my brother.'

Laura was about to plunge her hand into the soggy mass of toilet paper, but she straightened her back and turned around.

'Your brother is Robin Hood.'

John nodded. 'I pissed my mum off,' he explained. 'Moshe has taken my phone and laptop . . .'

Laura gave the smile she used when her kids begged for stuff they weren't going to get. 'I can't help you,' she said firmly.

'Please,' John begged. 'I have a watch my mum bought for my birthday. It's, like, two thousand pounds. It's never been out of the box and it's yours if you let me make a thirty-second call.'

Laura glanced about the spacious toilet cubicle as if she was looking for a hidden camera, and spoke stiffly. 'In line with Sherwood Resort policy, I keep all personal communications devices in my locker during working hours.'

'Eh?' John gasped.

Laura shook her head. 'Did Moshe Klein put you up to this?'

John was baffled. 'I don't know what you're talking about.'

'Three cleaners got fired for stealing when Moshe left valuables with tracking devices in guest rooms,' Laura said. 'If he wants to catch staff with mobile phones, he needs a maintenance issue that's less obviously fake.'

'Moshe is the one keeping me here.' John groaned. 'Laura, I swear on my dad's life. I'm a prisoner. There's a guard on the door, all the landlines and even the tellies have been taken away. *Please* let me send a message. How about I write it on a piece of paper with his email?'

Laura planted her hands on her hips. 'Mr Hood, or Kovacevic, or whatever your name is. I'm a single mother of two. I need this job, so please just let me scoop out whatever you've stuffed down this toilet.'

John felt bad putting Laura in such an awkward position. 'I'm sorry,' he said weakly as he backed into the hallway. His hands shook as he tucked them under his armpits and breathed deeply. In the toilet, Laura scooped wads of soggy tissue into the trash can.

John paced back towards his room, but after briefly deciding to give up, he thought about Moshe setting a trap for Robin and the rebels.

*I have to make this work.*

'What the—' Laura blurted as John charged into the toilet. Her gloved hand was full of soggy black napkins, and she flung them into John's face.

'Ugh!' John said, peeling a black lump out of his eye.

Laura looked scared and fumbled for something sharp in her tool bag.

'Don't come near me,' she warned.

But John was huge and fast. He dived on Laura, pinning her against the wall with one knee and wrapping a hand over her mouth so she couldn't scream.

'Don't be scared,' John said, almost tearful. 'I am so sorry, but Robin is in danger and I *have* to get in touch with him.'

Laura was on her own, with a man twice her weight restraining her.

'Get off!' she screamed, then tried to bite as John released his hand.

John thought about slapping Laura, or twisting her arm behind her back to stop her fighting, but even though he was desperate, the thought of hurting someone defenceless sickened him. All he could do was try to explain again.

'I need to get a message to Robin Hood,' he began. 'I am *begging* you to help me do that, but I won't hurt you, OK? I'm going to let you go. You're free to walk out of the door. Tell the guard what I did. My mum will send me to military school as punishment and Robin might get killed or captured. But it's up to you, OK?'

Laura studied John warily as he backed up to the opposite wall. Tears streaked down his face as he opened the door and signalled that she was free to go.

He was huge, but still not completely an adult. Laura pulled off the long glove and crawled to the door, then looked back warily as she picked up her tool bag and walked to the exit.

John felt hopeless and a huge lump rose up his throat as he backed down the hallway towards his room. But when Laura got close to the exit door and felt sure John had kept his promise to let her go, she hesitated.

'My twins are big Robin Hood fans,' she said, still wary. 'They've got T-shirts. They might not forgive me if he got caught.'

John sensed hope and smiled as Laura stepped back towards him.

'I wasn't lying when I said we have to leave our phones in our lockers,' Laura said, as she went down on one knee and took a battered phone handset with a long cable wound around it from her tool bag.

'This is my tester,' she explained. 'It generates pulses that we use to detect faults in the network cabling, but it can work like a regular phone. Dial hash-one-hundred-hash to get an external line.'

'Thank you *so* much,' John said, as he took it.

Laura sighed and looked worried as she headed back to finish pulling tissue out of the guest toilet. 'I just hope I don't live to regret helping you.'

# 34. DEFINITION OF STUPID

Robin went downstairs to a stressful scene in the Maid family den. The worst of Storm Verity had passed, but he felt shattered as Indio found him a clean T-shirt and soaked a cloth to wipe his bloody nose.

Matt was still tearful, and his younger brother Otto looked twitchy and kept asking if more roof was going to come down.

'It's getting too much,' Karma told her partner, as baby Zack grizzled on her shoulder. 'Maybe we can squat an empty house in Locksley.'

Indio sighed. 'It's freak weather. It will pass.'

'How long have they been saying that for?' Karma said, angry but keeping her voice low so she didn't wake the baby.

'I don't think it's safe,' Otto said pleadingly, as the seven-year-old gripped his mum around the waist.

'Stop going on about it,' Matt snapped at him. 'They'll inspect the roof tomorrow and there's nowhere else to go.'

With the Maid clan frightened and snapping at each other, Robin thought about going back to the command tent. But forwarding the virus had been his mistake, and he only had bad news about his attempts to hack the castle pump room, so he wasn't keen to face Jeanne and Will.

He glanced up as Marion came in, sweating and dusty from helping to clear the clinic.

'You OK, sweetie?' Indio asked.

'Gasping,' Marion said breathlessly.

She took a carton of orange from the fridge, and wasn't surprised when the light inside stayed off. Sherwood Outlets' electricity supply was flaky even when a storm hadn't just ripped a chunk of roof away.

'How many times? Don't drink from the carton!' Indio growled, as she opened a cabinet to give her a glass.

Robin felt his phone vibrate and felt a sense of dread, expecting to be summoned upstairs by Will. But it was a familiar voice on an unfamiliar number.

'Robin?' Little John gasped. 'Thank God!'

'You,' Robin said angrily. 'Those pictures you sent blew up my—'

'Moshe caught me,' John interrupted, before explaining how he was locked down, with a guard on the door and the dangling threat of Iwo Jima Military Academy.

Robin was even less keen to go up to the command tent now he had three pieces of bad news. But Moshe could be laying a trap, so the people planning to flood Sherwood Castle had to know straight away.

'That was Little John,' Robin told everyone. 'I have to go up top and speak to Will.'

'I'll come,' Marion said, before burping.

Indio looked furious. 'Young lady, it's chaos out there. And you two need to be careful. Security is focused on the emergency and you both have bounties on your heads.'

'My dad and thirty Brigands just arrived,' Marion explained. 'But I had to get a drink after breathing dust.'

Indio looked at Karma. 'We need to know what's going on. If I go up with the terrible twosome, will you watch the little ones?'

But Robin and Marion shot off while Indio put on wellies for the puddled roof. Someone had tied a ladder to replace the collapsed wooden stairs and Marion led them onto a roof where the weather had calmed, but the people hadn't.

A frightened, shouty crowd of seventy had gathered in front of the command tent. Will Scarlock stood on a wooden ammunition crate, shouting to be heard.

'You have to be realistic,' Will roared. 'I don't have all the answers right now. We'll inspect the roof tomorrow when it is light. I have a team working to restore electricity, but it's dark, there's standing water and they must put safety first.

'As for those spreading more elaborate theories, there is *no* evidence that the atrium roof collapse was caused by an explosion, or that Sheriff Marjorie's Castle Guards are massing for an imminent attack. We have enough problems without inventing fake ones.'

'What about water supply?' a woman shouted.

'There are newborn twins who don't have a tent in the parking lot, while long-term residents have entire stores with one or two families living in comfort,' a furious man added.

This comment caused ferocious debate in the crowd.

'Us long-term residents put years of labour into this mall,' a woman shouted. 'You take our emergency food, hot showers or medical care, and you call us selfish and ask for more.'

'So kids and cancer patients should live in a wet parking lot?' someone shouted back. 'While you have fridges and private bathrooms?'

Robin had never seen Will so close to losing control. Sam Scarlock shoved a woman when she tried to yank his father down off his crate, and Chicken Sheila scared people off with her mad eyes and a three-pronged fork crusted in bird poop.

'You know what the definition of stupid is?' Marion asked Robin, as they jogged towards the mayhem. 'A hundred people tightly packed next to a roof that just collapsed.'

'Your humour's getting darker,' Robin noted, as two mall security officers and several burly members of the Brigands Motorcycle Club forced their bodies between Will Scarlock and the surly crowd.

'Disperse!' the security team ordered. 'Meeting over.'

'Is that Cut-Throat?' Robin asked, as he noticed a statuesque, bearded figure standing back from the mob.

Marion saw him at the same moment and set off at a sprint before leaping into the giant biker's arms, yelling, 'Hey, Daddy-o!'

# 35. NO TIME LIKE THE PRESENT

Robin thought about saying hi to Cut-Throat, but decided to go in the command tent and get his shameful news out of the way.

Jeanne and Neo sat on one side of the big planning table, Unai, Azeem and Will's wife Emma on the other. Indio came in too and put a supportive arm around Robin as he delivered three pieces of bad news.

First, that he'd failed to find a quick method to hack Sherwood Castle's pump controls. Second, that the virus and two trashed laptops were his fault for being lazy and leaving his virus scanner switched off. Third, that Little John's spying had been unearthed by Moshe, who now knew they were interested in creating a flood by attacking the pump room.

'I'm sorry I let you all down,' Robin finished.

Unai was always moaning about Robin, but led his defence. 'You're a kid, we're grown-ups,' he said in a voice deepened by the tar from thousands of cigarettes. 'We look after you, not the other way around.'

There were nods from the other adults around the table and Indio squeezed Robin's shoulder, making him feel loved.

'Can you get in touch with your brother?' Neo Scarlock asked.

Robin nodded. 'Little John gave me an extension number and said he'll keep the test phone plugged in.'

'Do you think he'd be keen to help us again?' Azeem asked.

Robin shrugged. 'He probably wants to. But he's under guard and his all-access pass is history.'

Jeanne spoke next. 'When Moshe was messaging last night pretending to be Little John, did you talk about the pumps inside Sherwood Castle, or did you mention that we were also planning to take command of the dams upstream?'

Robin paused to think, then shook his head. 'I thought John was heading to school early Monday morning,' he said. 'So I kept it simple and asked for photos of the pump room.'

A wave of relief went around the table, which Robin didn't understand. He looked at Jeanne. 'You said flooding wouldn't damage the castle if the pumps were working. John heard Moshe say he'd disabled remote access to the pump room and put guards on the door.'

'I've been thinking about the system,' Unai answered. 'There's a third option, beside blowing up the pumps or hacking the controls.'

Robin smiled. 'Really?'

'Pumps need electricity,' Unai explained.

'So we cut the power lines?' Robin said enthusiastically.

Neo Scarlock nodded, then laughed. 'Do you want the good news or bad news first?'

'Good,' Robin said warily.

'Sherwood Castle is built on a floodplain, so mains electricity arrives by overhead cable,' Neo explained. 'All we have to do is climb a pylon and cut the cable. The bad news is that critical systems like flood defences are connected to a back-up diesel generator.'

'I've worked with generators,' Unai said. 'You only need two or three minutes' access to do serious damage.'

'We've studied the castle plans I downloaded,' Jeanne said. 'The generators are in an outbuilding, less than four hundred metres from your brother in the penthouse.'

Robin baulked. 'Why does Little John have to do it? When we hacked the StayNet system, we booked hotel rooms.'

'We thought about that,' Neo said. 'But the resort is running below ten per cent occupancy, which is barely one hundred guests. We know Moshe is on high alert and Sheriff Marjorie has recruited at least fifty new guards. So anyone booking into the hotel at short notice will be watched carefully.'

'And what about the guard?' Robin said.

Jeanne shrugged. 'We'll study the plans. There must be a way Little John can get out of the penthouse without the guard knowing.'

Robin didn't look convinced. 'He's not a climber like me. I've seen Little John turn to jelly on a two-metre diving board.'

'The only other option is to send in a team, all guns blazing,' Unai said. 'They might get to the generators, but they'll never make it out past two hundred Castle Guards.'

'We can't ask people to go on a suicide mission,' Azeem said.

'But we do have a friend in the Sheriff's office in Nottingham,' Neo added. 'Marjorie's chopper couldn't fly through the storm. She has early meetings tomorrow, so your brother will be home alone.'

'Wait!' Robin said, as the tent flaps opened behind him. 'You're talking about doing this *tonight*?'

Will Scarlock swept in, looking battered but determined, trailed by Sam, Chicken Sheila and Jake 'Cut-Throat' Maid, who ducked because he was giving Marion a piggyback.

'How's the angry mob?' Azeem asked.

'I've got four of my lads outside,' Cut-Throat said. 'Anyone trying to get in here will be sorry.'

'You can't perform miracles, Dad,' Neo said soothingly, as he took Will's wet coat and hung it up. 'Can I get you a rum to take the edge off?'

'No,' Will said strongly. 'We all need clear heads for this.'

'Why tonight?' Robin asked again. 'After everything we've been through today. We're knackered before we start.'

Will gave Robin a big smile, showing his rotten brown teeth. 'Many reasons,' Will began. 'We've gathered all the intelligence we need. The longer we wait, the greater the chance one of Marjorie's spies will find out what we're up to. Marjorie will want to show how tough she is before her presidential campaign kicks off. I have no evidence that her thugs are on their way here now, but it's only a matter of time.

'The last, and best, reason to act tonight is because, after everything we've been through with Storm Verity and the collapsed atrium roof, going on the attack is the last thing anyone will expect us to do.'

# 36. THE COCKTAIL CORRIDOR

Will was certain that Sheriff Marjorie had spies inside the mall, so he ordered the mission teams to assemble discreetly, away from main hallways and the crowd on the roof.

Team A was led by Lyla, along with Neo and a couple of trusted mall residents. Their job looked the simplest: hiking swampy ground towards the castle, locating an electricity pylon, climbing it and waiting for a signal to cut the power.

Team B was led by Jeanne, and would return by boat and road to the Control Centre at Darley Dale. Although they'd encountered no security at the dam that afternoon, there was a chance Moshe would beef things up once he realised there was more to the rebel plan than shutting off Sherwood Castle's pumps and hoping for a flood.

So Jeanne would set off with Sam Scarlock plus Cut-Throat Maid and a dozen Brigands who were riled up after the latest surge had destroyed their camp and prized motorbikes.

Indio was reluctant to let Marion join Team B, but Marion knew the area around the Control Centre after her earlier visit and her bow skills would be handy if they needed to take someone out silently. Cut-Throat made his ex-partner mad by saying Marion should come, and Marion followed the rule where she obeyed the parent whose decision suited her best.

Team C was led by security chief Azeem. They would stay back and defend Designer Outlets because Moshe and Sheriff Marjorie were unlikely to sit back and do nothing when a billion litres of water flushed through Sherwood Castle . . .

While the first three teams prepared their equipment and snuck out of the mall under cover of darkness, Team D had already begun work. Unai and Robin sat in Will's office at the back of the command tent with plans of Sherwood Castle and Robin's phone on speaker.

Inside the Sherwood Castle penthouse, Little John knelt over a display of plants inside the lobby, scraping decorative white pebbles into a nylon shoe bag. When it was half-full, he pulled the drawstring tight, hurried to his room and picked up the battered tester phone.

'I've got about two kilos of little stones,' he said.

'Nice,' Robin said. 'Did you find something sharp?'

'Easy,' John said. 'I ordered steak earlier, so I've got a big steak knife.'

They didn't have money growing up, and Robin remembered how steak was John's favourite and a rare treat.

'Bet you get steak every day now,' Robin said.

'Almost,' John admitted, then anxiously, 'Are you guys *sure* I can get out?'

Unai leaned over the dining table and spoke calmly at Robin's phone. 'John, the apartment has three bedrooms. I have a plan of your floor in front of me. I assume the master bedroom is your mother's. Is your bedroom next to that, or the one at the far end?'

'Far end,' John said.

'Is the middle bedroom locked?'

'No,' John said. 'I've hardly ever been in there. It's meant for guests, but Mum never has people to stay.'

'I need you to go in the middle bedroom,' Unai said. 'There's a walk-in wardrobe with a small utility cupboard at the back. Bring the fire extinguisher. I'll tell you what to do when you get there.'

'The cord on this phone isn't long enough,' John said. 'I'll have to plug in at another socket and call you back.'

'We're not in a hurry,' Unai said, knowing it would take a couple of hours for the team to reach the control room at Darley Dale and half an hour for any water they released to reach Sherwood Castle. 'Take your things and close the doors behind you, because you'll be making noise.'

Unai and Robin eyed each other as the line went dead. Two minutes passed before John called back.

'OK, the phone is plugged in in the guest room,' John said. 'I went through the walk-in wardrobe and I'm in the little cupboard. I didn't even know this was here.'

'What's in there?' Unai asked.

'Just a couple of boxes on the wall. Looks like a network switch and a fuse box.'

'Tap the wall at the back,' Unai said. 'It should sound hollow.'

John rapped and got the hollow sound.

'It's a sheet of drywall,' Unai said. 'Give it a good whack with the base of the fire extinguisher and it should break open.'

The cupboard didn't have enough space to take a swing while the door was closed, so John sat with his back braced against the door and launched a two-footed kick.

Robin jolted back from the desk as the bang came down the line. Little John slid his fingers between the cracked plaster and snapped off chunks to make a hole.

'There's yellow foam stuff inside a wooden frame and another board after that.'

'Pull the insulation foam out,' Unai said. 'Make sure there are no electrical wires, then do the same again to crack the drywall on the inside.'

John braced for another two-footed kick. He was surprised when, instead of making a hole, he ripped out nails holding the drywall to the wooden frame. The entire board tilted and hit the far wall of a narrow corridor.

'Blimey,' John said, as he coughed plaster dust.

'Can you escape?' Robin asked excitedly.

'Think so,' John said. He took his torch from a pocket and shone it through the hole into a long corridor. 'I had no idea this was back here.'

After a glance back through the spare bedroom and into the hallway to make sure the noise hadn't tipped off his guard, John wrapped the yellow insulation around a couple of jutting nails and pulled himself into a corridor. It was a metre wide and ran along the gently curved outer wall of the castle turret.

A couple of metres to John's right was a recess with a strip of commercial kitchen units, complete with microwaves, a big larder fridge, a pair of ovens and two serving trolleys. Further along was a big metal hatch, which would enable his mother to escape via the back of her closet if there was trouble, and a more normal-looking door at the end.

John realised this must open into the lounge, enabling waiting staff to heat snacks and serve drinks without tripping over guests in the grand lobby. It took another second to work out that he'd never noticed the door because the lounge curtains covered it.

In the other direction, the hallway went for fifteen metres, passing an ice machine. At the end was a waist-height lift designed for carrying food and a downward spiral staircase with *Mind Your Head* signs.

'Are you still with us?' Robin was asking, as John clambered back through his hole.

'I had no idea this was here,' John said. 'My mum *hates* parties, so it's probably never been used.'

Robin laughed. 'We went through several sets of plans. It's hidden on most of them. But on the original architect's drawing, it's called the Cocktail Corridor.'

Beyond the thrill of discovery and the satisfaction of getting one over on Moshe, John realised that this was only the start of something. His arms felt shaky as he backed into the spare room and sat on the bed.

'You can't keep stopping to plug a phone in the wall everywhere you go,' Unai said. 'So get a pen and pad. I'll tell you where you're going and what you need to do next.'

# 37. TWELVE ANGRY BRIGANDS

While most captains took a cautious approach on the Macondo River, wary of shallow water, bandit attacks and losing the river's path on flooded ground, the Brigands moved with the grace and delicacy of a sugared-up four-year-old with a hammer.

Their three fast boats had all been stolen from the Castle Guard. Where the river was wide enough they rode three abreast, with blazing searchlights and megaphones to shout at anyone who got in their way.

Fortunately, there was little traffic on the river at night, but Jeanne was horrified when their wash almost capsized a little boat carrying provisions to a forest settlement, while several Brigands laughed and hurled empty beer cans at their victim.

Marion had been around her father's gang her whole life. She was less shocked by the mayhem, but sensed that the loss of the Brigands' camp and dozens of prized motorbikes had wounded the gang's pride and made them more volatile and dangerous than ever.

'Dad, you need to calm them down,' Marion warned Cut-Throat, who stood at the wheel of the lead boat, wind blasting his beard and a beer in hand. 'If they're like this when we get near the dam, they'll hear us coming and bolt the doors.'

'Don't worry that dainty little head of yours,' Cut-Throat teased, as he flung his empty beer over the side.

'This isn't a joke,' Marion growled. 'And don't be so bloody sexist.'

Cut-Throat laughed. 'Tell your engineer pal to take a chill pill. And someone get me another beer before I kick all your asses!'

Two well-armed Brigands stayed back to guard the boats when they reached Old Road. They waded along flooded roads for half a kilometre to reach their meeting point, where Marion was alarmed to see ten more Brigands and three shabby open-backed trucks.

Everyone piled in the back of the trucks. Marion got squished between two bikers who hadn't washed in a while. She gripped the roll bar with both hands because Old Road was in terrible shape and the convoy's lead truck drove way above the speed limit.

After a few kilometres they passed an orange Forest Ranger truck coming the other way. The rangers inside weren't going to risk their lives for the sake of speeding tickets, and a Brigand in the last truck drew roars of laughter when he aimed a shotgun and tried to shoot out their back windscreen.

Jeanne thought things couldn't get worse, but after leaving Sherwood the convoy pulled off the highway and rolled into a retail park. It had a couple of drive-through restaurants and a builder's merchant stacked with bags of cement and piles of timber, but the last unit was a fancy, glass-fronted car dealership.

When Marion got close enough to see the sign, she read *Guy Gisborne Luxury Autos*.

As the trucks pulled up, the Brigands all jumped out and one guy used bolt cutters to snap the padlock on a metal entry gate.

'You know what to do!' Cut-Throat shouted.

As Brigands charged the car showroom, Jeanne approached Cut-Throat furiously, with Sam Scarlock as unenthusiastic back-up.

'This whole operation is carefully timed,' Jeanne began. 'Why have we stopped at a car dealership?'

Before Cut-Throat could answer, the lead truck accelerated up a short ramp, smashed its front bull bars into the dealership's glass lobby, and set off a chorus of alarms. The Brigands were known as expert vehicle thieves, and Marion watched as the driver of the truck booted the door of an office inside the showroom and used a crowbar to rip the door off a wall cabinet that held car keys.

Cut-Throat looked at Jeanne and Sam. 'I suppose you think we're a bunch of stupid thugs?' he asked irritably.

Jeanne took a half-step back, before Cut-Throat began an explanation. 'When Guy Gisborne finds out we've ripped off his motors, he'll hit the roof and send all his bent cops out to catch us. The second thing he'll do is get on the blower to Sheriff Marjorie and ask her Castle Guards and surveillance drones to do the same.

'So, my boys get some cars to chop for parts and earn money they desperately need after losing their bikes and homes. I also send a message to Gisborne that there are consequences if his goons chase my daughter through a hospital. And any guard or cop hunting bikers in stolen cars won't be on our backs when we're trying to get home after blowing the dams.'

Jeanne was relieved that there was logic in Cut-Throat's actions, and even a little impressed by his leadership skills. But Sam Scarlock looked annoyed as Brigands lined up in the showroom to take the keys for fancy cars.

'Has my father given you permission to do this?' Sam asked.

Marion knew that was the wrong thing to say, and winced as Cut-Throat poked Sam in the chest.

'I don't work for Will Scarlock,' Cut-Throat roared. 'We work together when our interests align.'

'Right,' Sam said, looking like he'd filled his underwear as Cut-Throat's beer breath washed over him.

'Daddy, calm down,' Marion said as she yanked Cut-Throat's denim waistcoat. 'Sam's a good guy.'

As a procession of Brigands drove shiny cars out of Guy Gisborne Luxury Autos, Cut-Throat led Sam, Marion and Jeanne over a grass embankment that separated the retail park from the main road.

Two fresh pickup trucks were parked on the kerb, but these had double cabs so everyone could ride inside, and the four bikers standing beside them seemed calm, well equipped and mostly sober. Marion even recognised one of them and welled up at the surprise.

'Diogo!' She beamed as she recognised the Portuguese biker she'd lived with over the summer. 'How's the delta? Have you proposed to Napua yet?'

As Marion hugged Diogo, he reached over her head and shook Cut-Throat's hand.

'Thanks for sorting trucks and getting here at short notice,' Cut-Throat said. 'I love my gang, but most of 'em are maniacs and this needs subtlety.'

'Always got your back, Cut-Throat,' Diogo said. 'The surges clog waterways and kill wildlife in the delta, so this is our problem too.'

Marion settled in the back of the first truck, between Jeanne, who seemed more confident about how things were going, and Sam, who'd heard rumours about how Jake 'Cut-Throat' Maid had earned his nickname and was still trembling.

A Brigand in a stolen Porsche made a victory sign as he blasted by, then Diogo pulled into traffic and kept at a sensible speed, the second truck right behind. They'd driven a kilometre when two police drones zoomed overhead. Then came an epic boom and an orange fireball lit up the sky behind them.

As chunks of the Guy Gisborne Luxury Autos building spiralled through the air, Cut-Throat looked back at Marion from the passenger seat and gave her a big smile. 'If Gisborne's people come after you again, it'll be something more painful than his car showroom that gets torched . . .'

# 38. THE LOOMING THREAT

Little John reached the bottom of the spiral stairs and pushed a green mushroom-shaped button to release a door. He didn't feel great, because he'd never met the gruff foreign-sounding guy who'd given him instructions, and neither Unai nor Robin seemed to appreciate that it was hard moving around Sherwood Castle without a card to open doors.

After peeking to make sure nobody was around, John stepped into a windowless room with scuffed white walls and grey vinyl floor tiles. The door he'd just come through had a touchpad lock on the outside, so he balled two sheets from his notebook and packed them into the latch-hole so it didn't lock behind him.

John was now on the floor that had conference rooms and his mother's office. He'd exited into a staff area. The lights were on and there were three trolleys with platters of little sandwiches. A function was under way in a room down the hallway, its lively chatter dominated by a horrifying fake laugh.

John had to get out before someone came by. He pushed on a set of double doors, which he assumed would lead to an empty conference room. They were locked, so he tapped the battered card he'd found in his mum's bedroom but wasn't surprised that it didn't work.

He started along a service corridor, hoping to find an exit into a public part of the resort, but a waitress in a black and white uniform came from the busy meeting room and heard his footsteps.

'Steve?' she said. 'Didn't I tell you to go on break before we start coffee and dessert?'

John, who had reached a dead end, turned back to the nervous waitress. She'd not seen John before, but he shared his mother's looks and bulk, so it didn't take a genius to figure out who he was.

'Always wondered where that door led,' the waitress said awkwardly.

John gawped and felt like he ought to say something. He could flatten the waitress if she yelled, but Moshe didn't want rebel spies finding out he was a captive, so hopefully she had no reason to be suspicious.

'I was heading to the gym,' John said, which tied in with his tracksuit and backpack. 'But my access card has died.'

'I've replaced my card three times.' The waitress sighed. 'Typical King Corp. Everything done on the cheap.'

The waitress gawped like she'd said the wrong thing, and John smiled.

'I won't grass you up to my mum,' he joked, as the woman pulled a card tied to her skirt.

'Which way do you need to go?' she asked.

'Any public area, so I can get down to the gym.'

'You'll need to tap again to get in the gym, but they'll swap your card at reception.'

The waitress let John out through the empty conference room. People in suits paid no attention to him as he waited for the lift, and he entered a staff corridor on the first floor by cursing his useless card until an old geezer carrying a mop let him through.

John didn't need to do the same at the opposite end, because a truck was backed up to an open shutter and pallets of fruit and veg were being wheeled to a service lift.

The wind bit and puddles splashed as John crunched over gravel in the dark, crossing a service lot with tractors, equipment sheds and a row of limousines that had been mothballed when resort business took a downturn.

The generator was easy to spot because it was built on a raised plinth to prevent flooding. It comprised a two-storey diesel tank, shaped like a soft drink can, and the generator alongside in a ridged metal cabin.

John halted as he closed in and got caught in a motion-sensing floodlight. Luckily, nobody else was around, but it was another uncomfortable reminder that he was following a plan made on paper from twenty kilometres away.

Dangerously slippy moss covered the narrow steps up to the generator. The floodlight was situated for tankers delivering fuel. It went out as he walked up the steps and reached the hut's narrow metal door.

There was no touchpad, just an old-fashioned lock wanting a key. Unai said he wouldn't need to force the lock, because generators run hot and there would be windows that opened and removable exterior panels for mechanics to replace large parts.

But Unai's instructions weren't precise, and John's heartbeat was lively as he crept around the building shining his torch.

The best way in seemed to be a plastic side window, big enough to get through and held in place with flimsy plastic catches. John levered one corner with a thumbnail and dug the steak knife into the gap, but then orange warning lamps from a dustcart flicked along the hut and he had to squat down until the cart reached dumpsters at the far end of the compound.

John gripped the solid metal steak knife with both hands. It took all his strength to twist the blade sideways until a catch holding the window snapped. The sound sent a low boom through the metal wall, but the second catch was easier because he could get his fingers inside.

After a glance to make sure the bin collectors weren't heading back, John posted his backpack into the hut then pulled himself inside after it. There was a light switch by the door, but with windows along each side he decided it was safest to rely on his torch.

The space had a new plastic smell and a control cabinet operated by touchscreen. The generator ran along the back wall of the hut, comprising a beefy twelve-cylinder diesel engine with its drive shaft connected to an electrical generator.

Once John got his bearings, he remembered Unai's instructions and sought the fuel line from the adjacent tank. He used his torch to follow this pipe up to the cylinder head atop the engine, where the distributor sent fuel to each cylinder.

In front of the distributor was a bulging blue cylinder with a handle. A wraparound sticker said **TO ISOLATE FILTER, TWIST HANDLE UNTIL YOU HEAR A CLICK.**

John twisted, heard the click, and was surprised when the entire blue assembly popped out and dripped fuel that ran down the back of his hand towards his wrist. He needed both hands for the next step, so he wiped his hand on his tracksuit bottoms and trapped the torch between his neck and shoulder.

Inside the blue drum was a cylindrical plastic filter, designed to catch rust or dirt that could do serious damage if it got sucked inside the engine. Unai said the engine would have a sensor and wouldn't switch on if the filter was removed entirely, so John put the steak knife inside the filter and dragged it up and down, shredding the plastic mesh.

Next, John took the drawstring shoe bag from his backpack and filled the torn filter with the gritty white stones he'd scraped off the planters in the penthouse.

Unai reckoned the stones would get sucked into the engine the moment it fired up, clogging the distributor and damaging the piston seals in a way that would take hours to fix.

The orange lights from the departing dustcart flashed across the walls as John slotted the sabotaged filter back in place. Finally he cleared away a few stones he'd dropped, and felt satisfied as he pulled a length of tissue from a wall-mounted dispenser to wipe the smelly diesel fuel off his fingers.

There was nobody around as he climbed back out of the window, and he hooked one broken catch back in place so his break-in looked less obvious. John was set to go down the steps when he heard an approaching helicopter.

His first thought was that his mum had changed her mind about coming home now the storm had passed, but the sound was too deep to be the helicopter she usually used, and there were two sets of flashing lights in the sky, a few hundred metres apart.

These large helicopters were too beefy for the seventh-floor helipad, and used a row of landing pads a couple of hundred metres from where John currently stood. Even when Sherwood Castle Resort was doing well, these big choppers only came in once or twice a week, delivering high-end wedding parties and gamblers.

As the noise of the approaching choppers escalated, John decided to climb the metal ladder on the side of the fuel tank to see what was going on. The brilliantly lit landing pads glowed over a thick hedge as he reached the top rung.

John counted forty-something Castle Guards standing near the pads or sitting on equipment packs. All wore combat gear rather than the tweed suits they wore on duty inside the resort. There were also three large military drones prepped for launch and a fourth in bits being attended by a mechanic.

'That's not good,' John told himself as he slid down the ladder.

He'd brought the test phone along in his backpack, and he knew he had to find the nearest socket and let Robin know what he'd seen.

# 39. READING MOSHE KLEIN

Robin charged into the command tent and told Emma and Will Scarlock about the drones and choppers being prepped at Sherwood Castle.

'At least we know what's coming,' Will said.

'But not where,' Emma cautioned, looking up from the planning table.

'At least John's confident that the generator is sabotaged,' Robin said. 'He was in a store room when he spoke to me. He's hoping to get back in the penthouse before the guard realises he's gone.'

'Some good news at least,' Will said. He approached one of his whiteboards with details of the four teams and wrote *TASK COMPLETE* next to Team D.

'Azeem is already doing all she can to prepare for a possible attack here,' Emma said, as she studied a map of the forest. 'But we need to alert the team heading for Darley Dale to be on the lookout for drones and choppers.

'I also think it's time to tip off the media,' Emma continued. 'Marjorie wants to be president, but her get-tough rhetoric will blow up in her face if her private army gets out of hand while cameras are watching.'

'Good thinking,' Will agreed.

Robin spoke next. 'I brought this up from my den,' he said, placing a gadget in a plastic food box on the table. 'I built it to jam police drones. It probably won't work against military drones, but no harm trying.'

'I'll pass it up to the lookouts in the watchtower,' Will said.

'Also, when I was running up here, I noticed heaps of refugees leaving the parking lot and heading for the forest,' Robin continued. 'I guess the roof collapse and seeing Azeem preparing for an attack has scared them off.'

'We've done all we can to help as many people as we can.' Emma sighed.

'Godspeed to them,' Will added.

'If you don't need me for anything else, I'll go back to my den,' Robin said. 'Get my bow and arrows and some other gear.'

'Keep safe,' Emma warned.

'Let us know straight away if you hear more from Little John,' Will said, then as an afterthought he threw Robin a walkie-talkie. 'Take this, it's fully charged.'

The night was cool and Robin's breath curled in front of his face as he stepped out of the tent. There was no sign of the rooftop mob from earlier, but several teams worked around the damaged roof, dragging debris and tipping market stalls on their sides to make defensive positions along the roof's edge.

Robin looked up at the moon and got a chill down his back. He sensed that everything would be different when the sun rose in a few hours' time.

The route back to his den had changed. The long-term residents had reluctantly agreed to let the neediest refugees into the northern legs of the mall, and the hallway was suddenly loud and full of people fighting over the best spots.

Dr Gladys's clinic had relocated to the bookstore that usually served as a school, but Robin's biggest shock came when he reached his den and found that he now shared it with Cut-Throat's heavily tattooed girlfriend Liz, her two little kids and a bull terrier named Psycho.

'Indio and Karma said we could bunk here till things got sorted,' Liz said.

'Of course,' Robin said, knowing it was the right thing to do, but resenting the invasion of the cosy little den he'd got used to sharing with Marion.

Psycho sniffed Robin's boot and Marion's half-brother toddled around in a nappy singing a song about a moo cow as Robin found his bow, then stepped onto a chair to reach the high shelf, where a brick of M112 demolition explosive had been stored since summer.

'Marion's nicked half my good arrows,' Robin complained, as he sat at the table preparing six arrows with explosive and detonators, then added, 'It's not plasticine,' as little hands made a grab.

While Robin made six explosive arrows and filled his backpack with a canteen of water, some chocolate, a hunting knife, a stun gun and the night-vision goggles he'd liberated from the Castle Guard a couple of days earlier, Psycho peed on the floor, one of the kids ripped a book and Liz rummaged through the mini-fridge and complained there was no beer.

'Me and Marion aren't big drinkers,' Robin said resentfully. 'And maybe wipe up the dog pee before your three-year-old walks through it.'

As he headed down the escalator, Robin suspected he'd get a better night's sleep in Sheila's chicken sheds than with Cut-Throat's nutty family. He tried not to think about the horrors of his new domestic set-up as he took his walkie-talkie, ducked under the metal shutter and stepped out of the sports store.

'This is Robin,' he told the radio. 'Ready for action. Where do you want me?'

# 40. THAT ANNOYING KAREN

While cops went after Brigands in stolen cars, the two pickups heading for the control room at Darley Dale were licensed, insured, and stayed under the speed limit. The Brigands riding in the front of the second truck were brothers in their forties named Jurgen and Felix.

'Met Felix in juvenile detention when we were thirteen years old,' Cut-Throat said, as Marion and the other occupants of the lead truck watched Felix walk to the heavy gate of the dam's approach road. 'Older kids tried to bully us, so we broke into the kitchen and stole meat cleavers . . .'

'Great to have a parent who sets a positive example,' Marion said cheekily.

It took Felix seconds to open the locked gate with a bump key. The two-truck convoy rolled through.

'No sign of Castle Guards or choppers,' Diogo said.

Cut-Throat grunted. 'If they know why we're here, they'll lay an ambush around the control room. So let's not walk into it.'

After driving two of the three kilometres to the hilltop at speed, they pulled up. Diogo hurriedly uncovered the pickup bed, revealing a cache of grenades, assault rifles and extra arrows for Marion.

The second truck held a similar cargo, with the addition of a tripod-mounted M2HB machine gun and a metal case filled with strings of 50mm ammo.

'Nice gear!' Cut-Throat said. 'How'd you get this stuff so fast?'

Diogo smiled. 'Don't move weapons myself, but I know every smuggler in the delta.'

'Never bring a knife to a gunfight,' a stocky little Brigand called Mike said cheerfully, handing Sam an assault rifle. 'You good with that, kid?'

When they resumed the uphill drive, the big tripod gun was mounted on the rear platform of the second truck, and Sam and Cut-Throat stood in the bed of the lead pickup with weapons ready and a thermal camera to pick up any signs of movement. Marion had more arrows than she could carry and Jeanne had reluctantly agreed to wear a holster with an automatic pistol.

Sam kept scanning the landscape, but the only heat signatures came from birds and a herd of resting sika deer.

'Wherever Marjorie's choppers went, it wasn't here,' Diogo said when they rolled up beside the Control Centre.

Felix and Cut-Throat headed for the grand but dilapidated entrance, with Diogo, Sam and Jurgen giving cover. Mike manned the big gun in the back of the pickup and Jeanne squatted beside the pickup, giving Marion final instructions on what they needed to do at the control console.

Felix discovered that control room staff locked the door at night, but had no bother forcing it open. Cut-Throat was first into the control room, and gave the guy at the console doing a sudoku puzzle the fright of his life.

'Where's your pal?' Cut-Throat asked.

As the controller studied the scary men with guns, he held up both hands and pointed with a pinkie finger. 'Karen's in her office doing reports.'

Felix backed out of the control room and looked down the corridor. 'Which door?'

'Second left,' the controller shouted.

Felix ran to the office and found the door locked.

'Karen, we're not here to hurt you,' Felix said, as he realised the door frame was rotten and barged it with his shoulder.

The wood around the door hinges split and the heavy panelled door slammed open, revealing a spacious office with a huge wooden map of the Macondo dam system on the back wall.

'Come on,' Felix urged, searching for Karen under the desk and in the gap between two file cabinets.

A breeze rattled the papers on the desk, and Felix tracked its source to a circular window, partly obscured by an old-fashioned coat stand.

Felix took out his walkie-talkie. 'One of 'em got out,' he said. 'Female controller out window at the rear. See if she comes around for her car.'

'Have eyes on the cars,' Sam answered. 'No sign of her.'

Felix looked out of the window and saw a figure running away, but he made a hash of going after her, with his belt loop catching on the window clasp and stuff spilling from pockets as he pulled himself outside.

By the time Felix was on his feet, Sam had run around to meet him.

'Saw her disappear,' Sam said, pointing along the road leading to the massive dam. 'Fast and fit.'

'Damn!' Felix shouted as he bent over picking up coins and lock picks.

Karen was too far away to chase, so they met up with Marion and Jeanne around the front.

'It probably takes three or four minutes to run to the dam from here,' Jeanne said. 'There might be an emergency phone.'

'Or her mobile,' Marion added. 'If there's a signal out here.'

'How long for your business in the control room?' Sam asked.

'Two minutes to set the controls and start releasing water here,' Jeanne said. 'Six and a half for the water from here to reach Youlgreave, then four minutes with water spilling from both dams. Then we shut everything off and head home.'

'We need two releases combining in the eastern river channel to really hammer Sherwood Castle,' Marion explained, remembering what she'd learned playing with Jeanne's 3D model.

'Call it fifteen minutes total,' Sam said. 'Let's hope we can last that long before anyone shows up.'

Marion lined up beside Jeanne at the ornate mechanical console. There was a bleep as Jeanne started a fifteen-minute countdown on her fitness watch.

'Marion, the four green channel switches over your head need to be in the down position. Watch the flow gauges and let me know if pressure goes into the red.'

'Right, boss,' Marion said as she flipped switches.

Jeanne set a bunch of dials, then pulled the master control lever. A flickering bulb came on beneath a warning sign, and after a loud clunk the ninety-year-old console came to life with cogs, control wires and hissing hydraulics.

A red light began flashing overhead, and a row of dusty filament bulbs flickered on a wooden indicator board at the side of the room, showing five gates pouring water down the Darley Dale's eastern slipway. This was followed by a foghorn blast that made everything vibrate.

'What was that?' Cut-Throat yelled over the noise.

'Warning horn,' Jeanne explained. 'Gates are opening.'

'Two hundred thousand litres per second,' Marion said as she watched the gauges. 'Five hundred thousand, nine hundred thousand.'

'OK,' Jeanne said, rubbing her hands and mostly talking to herself. 'We open the gates at Youlgreave in six minutes. Activate the emergency signal to warn shipping and start setting the controls.'

'Eight million and rising,' Marion told her dad happily, as the horn blasted down the valley in front of the dam. 'That's three swimming pools per second!'

# 41. THE CLEAN SHOT

There were screams and shouts as refugees escaping Sherwood Outlets saw the three large drones buzz over treetops. Travelling at 130 kmh, the trio reached the mall thirty seconds later. Two screamed left while the lead drone went for the wooden watchtower.

Moshe's spies had told him that the tower and command tent below were the hub of Will Scarlock's organisation. A rebel guard in the tower heard the drones blast out of the night and flicked Robin's jamming device, more in hope than expectation. Her two colleagues snatched guns to take a shot.

Robin had taken up position on one of the southern spokes of the roof, close to the chicken sheds, with Neo Scarlock for company and rows of angled solar panels to hide behind.

'Biggest drone I've ever seen!' Neo gasped, craning his neck as it got loud. 'It's gonna—'

Before he could say *hit*, the drone completed its suicide mission, smashing into the wooden tower at full speed with a small, but devastating, payload of explosives.

At least two rebels were engulfed in fire as they jumped off the tower.

'My parents are in the tent,' Neo said, shielding his face from the heat as he began to sprint towards the explosion.

Robin thought about following, but then the roof shook so violently that Neo was knocked off his feet. He slumped over a solar panel. Glass panes shattered in the greenhouses where the rebels grew vegetables, and the dome hanging over the atrium made a further groaning tilt towards doom.

As Neo stumbled to his feet holding his gashed arm, one of the two drones that had broken left skimmed across the rooftop, spitting out little chunks that fizzed on contact with the air and burst into blue-white flame when they landed.

Robin notched an explosive arrow and tried to track the drone, but it was too fast. A trio of rebels at the edge of the roof had a better angle, with the drone coming straight at them.

Twin shotgun blasts threw up pellets which shredded the drone as it passed through. As the drone spiralled out of control and slapped down in the flooded car park, the chunks continued to burn white hot, blackening and melting the roof.

Robin's head barely reached the tops of the solar panels, but he could see people rushing to the greenhouses.

'We think it's phosphorous,' a breathless woman warned Robin as she jogged past holding a sack of soil. 'If that gets on your skin, it'll burn down to the bone.'

Neo resumed his run to the command tent, but Robin felt useless as he watched people scoop greenhouse soil into anything that would hold it and dump it on the phosphorus fires. Most were easily extinguished, but several pieces of the highly reactive compound had dropped down a vent near the roof's edge, and a tongue of flame shot from its grille.

A frantic chicken shot past Robin as he moved towards the smouldering wreckage of the watchtower and command tent. As he jogged, the third drone flickered across the face of the moon. It had settled into a high position, circling and relaying pictures of the damage back to Moshe at Sherwood Castle.

There were more loose chickens, but Sheila was handling them, stapling wire mesh over a wooden panel that had been knocked loose by the blast. One rebel guard had broken her leg jumping from the tower and Will had minor burns on the back of his hands from dragging gear out of the blazing tent, but they were the only injuries Robin could see.

'We need volunteers,' Unai shouted to anyone who'd listen. 'Get water from the shower block. If the fire spreads through the vents, we'll lose the entire southern roof.'

There were plenty of people, but no obvious way to get water across the roof.

'Sheila's got a water supply in the chicken sheds,' Robin said. 'And a pressure hose we use to muck out.'

As Unai led volunteers towards the sheds, Azeem's voice came out of their walkie-talkies.

'I'm by the river and we've spotted a helicopter,' Azeem said. 'There's no obvious landing spot, but plenty of shallow water where guards can jump out.'

Robin decided he was more useful shooting than firefighting and headed for the nearest barricade.

'Hey!' Marion's brother Matt yelled as Robin turned and clattered into him. Robin was surprised to see Marion's ten-year-old brother carrying a bow, a backpack and ten of Robin's best carbon core arrows.

'No wonder I've got no ammo,' Robin said furiously. 'First Marion's swiping my arrows, now you.'

'These are mine,' Matt said.

This was an obvious lie, because there were a hundred different types of arrow on the market and these were the exact ones Robin was missing.

'Your mums will be worried,' Robin said irritably. 'Go back to the den.'

Matt scowled determinedly. 'I'm as big as you.'

'You're *ten*,' Robin said, taking a deep breath so that his muscular frame swelled. 'You may be tall, but I can flip you like a pancake.'

'I can't sit down there,' Matt said. 'Waiting to get crushed like Jasprit did.'

Robin remembered how upset Matt had been, and felt for him.

'Finn's screaming, Otto's in meltdown, Karma and Indio are fighting,' Matt continued. 'It's doing my head in.'

'You boys OK?' Emma Scarlock asked as she approached, Will a couple of steps behind, a wet cloth wrapped around his burnt fingers.

'Matt won't go back to the den,' Robin said. 'And he's nicked half my good arrows.'

'Snitch,' Matt growled.

'We've got plenty of adults up here,' Emma said. 'Maybe it's best if you boys *both* went inside and helped look after your family.'

None of them knew that the circling drone had kept eyes on Will Scarlock since he'd charged out of the burning tent. Now its pilot saw Robin too – and a chance to kill the two most important rebels in a single strike.

# 42. FOUR MINUTES THIRTY

'Time for Youlgreave Dam,' Jeanne said with composure, looking at the countdown on her watch.

Marion flipped two switches on the mechanical console. Jeanne pulled a lever and bulbs lit on the wooden indicator board:

> **YOULGREAVE EMERGENCY GATE No. 1 – *OPEN***
> **YOULGREAVE EMERGENCY GATE No. 2 – *OPEN***

'Four minutes thirty before we can switch off and clear out,' Jeanne told Cut-Throat, as the giant biker kept one eye on the captive controller.

'Good stuff,' Cut-Throat said cheerfully.

Outside was calm too. Mike manned the big gun on the pickup bed, Diogo used binoculars to watch insane amounts of water blasting down the dam's eastern slipway, Felix smoked a cigarillo and his brother Jurgen peed against a tree.

Sam stood at the highest point of the road, scanning with the thermal camera. All seemed calm, until he saw a small orange smear on his display. 'Cars,' Sam announced, zooming in. 'At least two.'

Weapons clicked and Jurgen zipped his fly. The blurs on Sam's screen moved rapidly and were soon close enough that he ought to see headlights. And you only switch headlights off if you don't want to be seen . . .

'Definitely hostile, closing fast,' Sam shouted.

The nineteen-year-old made an easy target atop the hill, so he backed towards some bushes as Mike eagerly swung the tripod-mounted gun towards the road.

'Taste this, ya wombats!' Mike yelled.

But the first shot came from behind him – a rifle round that missed Diogo by less than a metre. It ripped through the radiator of the lead pickup, which was still hot enough to erupt in a hiss of steam.

Diogo tried lunging towards Sam, but switched direction as bullets tracked him across the road. His only option was to dive under the truck, but he knew a stray bullet hitting the ammo stored overhead would be the end of him.

Sam ducked as shots ripped up the bush he hid in. Felix sighted the group running up from the dam and opened fire. Mike blasted the big gun the other way and blew something up, but before he figured what, he was caught by a searchlight in the sky and swung the gun up to aim wildly at a helicopter skimming overhead.

'We've got company!' Felix shouted into the Control Centre, though Marion, Jeanne and Cut-Throat had already heard the gunfire.

'We need three minutes,' Jeanne shouted back.

Felix got shot in the calf, landing on marble paving in front of the Control Centre's main door as bullets cracked in from all directions. A single round from Mike's heavy gun had obliterated one of the cars coming up the hill, and the ones behind had stayed well out of shooting range.

Diogo crawled around beneath the damaged pickup and aimed his binoculars. He saw at least two police cars and an armoured riot van down the hill, while several dam staff and Castle Guards came from the other direction. Mike was still using the big gun to shoot recklessly at a helicopter now way out of range, so Diogo crawled to the second truck and yelled at him.

'Mike, look for cops circling around on foot,' he ordered. 'Everyone else, focus on the guys coming up from the dam.'

Sam heard Diogo's orders, but was frozen in shock after twenty bullets had shredded the bushes all around him without landing a hit. Jurgen was more interested in his injured brother than in battle tactics, and almost got shot in the arse as he ran to help.

Inside the Control Centre, Cut-Throat opened the main door and helped Jurgen drag Felix inside.

'Let me stay and shut off the water,' Jeanne yelled from the control room as Cut-Throat returned. 'Barricade the doors, and the rest of you can leave.'

'Can't you leave the dam gates open?' Cut-Throat asked.

'Too little and we won't flood the castle. Too long and we'll cause massive flooding and danger to life downstream.'

'We can't leave a man behind!' Marion said determinedly.

But with Sam too scared to move, Mike and Diogo holding back the cops downhill and everyone else inside the Control Centre, the group coming up from the dam faced zero resistance. One burly Castle Guard already had his back to the wall next to the main door of the Control Centre.

'Don't come out the front door,' Sam warned over the radio. 'The guards have you covered.'

'Dammit!' Cut-Throat boomed, as he booted a chair and sent the controller flying out of it. 'I'd rather shoot my way out than go back to prison.'

'Two minutes,' Jeanne said, then spoke quietly to Marion. 'What about that side window the other controller used?'

Cut-Throat was cursing Sam over the radio for not shooting at Castle Guards, Felix was shot and Jurgen was a headless chicken, torn between shooting, surrendering and helping his injured brother.

'This is a shambles!' Marion told Jeanne as she grabbed her bow and backpack.

'Head straight for home,' Jeanne whispered fondly. 'You know the forest better than any of us.'

Marion slipped out of the control room without her dad noticing. A bullet splintered the front door as she sprinted down the hallway and found the office with the round window.

After putting her face up to the glass to make sure all the carnage was around the front, Marion dropped her bow and backpack outside then slid out herself. She heard Cut-Throat yell, 'Where did my daughter go?' but didn't go back to explain.

Despite Jeanne's advice, Marion had no intention of running away. After making sure her walkie-talkie was muted, Marion crawled along the side of the Control Centre, accompanied by another warning blast from the dam and an ear-shattering barrage from the big gun holding off the cops.

As Marion neared the action, she scampered to a boulder sticking out of the rugged terrain and stifled a gasp as she knelt in a deep puddle.

There wasn't much moonlight, but the Castle Guards were flashing torches and the dam workers had reflective stripes on their orange boiler suits.

Marion buried her face as the helicopter skimmed over and started dropping down to land. They were already outnumbered by cops and guards, so the idea of another twenty or thirty arriving was scary. But the big gun had forced the chopper to land further away, which at least bought them some time . . .

# 43. ROBIN HURTS HIS BUM

Robin felt like he was in a movie.

He saw his life flash before him: from the first arrow he'd notched at six years old. The calloused fingers, the push-ups and pull-ups he'd done to strengthen his arms and chest, the online videos showing how to shoot fast, the running, the climbing. The hours he'd spent shooting bullseye after bullseye until the centre of his target disintegrated.

Now a seventy-kilo explosive-packed suicide drone was bearing down on him at a hundred kilometres per hour. Not much light, a slight breeze. Shoot too soon, he might miss. Leave it too late, he'd risk getting caught in the explosion.

Robin saw his mum calling him to heaven, saw Marion riding a zebra and his body being carried through Locksley in a casket in front of thousands of crying mourners. Or the bits of it that had been scraped off the roof after the explosion . . .

*Stop thinking crazy thoughts, dumbass.*

*Have they knocked my old house down yet?*

*Which pocket did I put my phone in?*

But at this speed, Robin's conscious brain was barely involved. It was all muscle memory. Explosive arrow notched, pull back, aim, release.

A perfect shot.

The explosive arrow hit the drone left of centre. As the tip speared the drone's body, the arrow's tail snapped off and got sucked through one of the drone's four propellers. A hundred thousand pounds' worth of technology jerked off course and ripped apart as it spun end over end.

There were people all over the roof, and they yelled as chunks of drone smashed down. The biggest crashed into the hanging glass dome.

After a creak of metal it went through several tonnes of glass and crashed down into the atrium. Purely by luck, Robin's arrow had separated the detonator from the drone's package of explosives, so nothing blew up.

'What was that?' Will gasped, having not even seen it coming.

'Shot!' Emma told Robin, then to her husband, 'He just saved our lives.'

Dust rose out of the atrium. Unai's frantic firefighting team kept working.

As Robin lowered his bow, his back foot stepped awkwardly on a ridge between two sections of roof and his moment of triumph ended with him knocking Matt down and Robin's bum getting spiked by an arrow that stuck out of Matt's backpack.

'Oww!' Robin yelled, rolling onto his side and hissing.

The arrow had only made a tiny cut, but the tip was snagged in his tracksuit bottoms and it swung between his legs as Emma gave him a hand up.

'OK?' she asked.

'Had worse,' Robin said, rubbing his bum and realising his legs were soaking wet.

Azeem came over the radio, sounding more worried than before. 'We've got eyes on Castle Guards jumping out of a chopper into the river and a second chopper is closing in. I've got defensive positions set up, but if anyone is available we'd appreciate extra help down here.'

'Roger that,' Will answered. 'I'm afraid we've got every spare body fighting fires.'

'I'll go,' Robin announced, and ran before Emma could get involved.

The usual way down from the roof was via stairs or ladder, but the quickest was the ropes used to haul goods up on market day.

'Don't shoot me in the back!' Robin told four Arab women as he ran by.

They usually ran a stand that made tagine pasties and Moroccan flatbreads, but were presently armed with machine guns and grenades. They had their serving table as a shield and their firing positions defended with sacks of flour.

'Careful, Robin,' the youngest woman warned, as he fearlessly gripped a frayed rope and checked the pulley.

'Azeem says the river beyond the southern parking lots is off limits,' another added. 'It's been booby-trapped.'

'Good to know,' Robin said, as he gave a cheeky salute and hopped off the roof.

Gripping the rope tightly, he swung out and walked down the wall. To his surprise, Matt grabbed a rope further along and used a more reckless technique, wrapping his legs around the rope to slide down and reaching the lapping water at the edge of the parking lot before Robin.

'You're taking the mickey!' Robin said, giving Matt a shove. 'Emma told you to go back to your family.'

'Emma told *both* of us to go back. And Marion always says you wouldn't last five minutes if she didn't have your back.'

Robin tutted. 'She does, does she?'

'No way I'm going back inside,' Matt said.

Robin thought about old movies, where the hero takes out an annoying or disrespectful character with a single knockout punch. But he doubted it was that easy in real life, and even if he did knock Matt out, he'd then have to carry the annoying brat to safety . . .

'If you fall off the wall, I'm not pulling you out,' Robin said.

'I've seen you swim.' Matt smirked. 'I'm not the one who's gonna drown.'

The first of the two big helicopters was lifting off, which meant thirty Castle Guards were on the ground and Robin didn't have time to argue.

'Just . . . Do whatever!' Robin snapped, before setting off.

# 44. TIMMY SQUIRREL BITES THE DUST

Marion saw clear ground ahead and sprinted behind another rock that gave a better view over the Control Centre entrance. The four Castle Guards had neater uniforms than the bikers, but seemed equally clueless, while the two dam workers had worried eyes and held their rifles the way Marion held Zack when his nappy leaked.

An athletic female guard in a Kevlar helmet stood in a ridiculously open position arguing tactics with a taller man, while the guard in front of the Control Centre glanced about with body language that Marion interpreted as *Are you dicks gonna stand there arguing until someone comes out and shoots me?*

As the helicopter landed several hundred metres away, Marion stealthily notched an arrow and took aim. Her first shot speared through the athletic guard's body armour, and while Marion hadn't mastered Robin's trick of holding multiple arrows, she still unleashed two more fast enough to shoot the big dude and the guard poised by the Control Centre entrance as he swung his rifle to shoot back.

'It's Robin Hood!' one of the orange-clad dam workers blurted before they both ran away.

Marion couldn't know if there were more guards or cops in hiding, but Sam stood to give her cover now she'd done the hard work. Marion ran to the Control Centre entrance, feeling like a terrible person as the guy she'd shot near the door writhed and coughed up blood.

As Marion ripped his gun away, the helicopter took off. This seemed weird, because she couldn't imagine a platoon of Castle Guards and their equipment disembarking so fast. But she was in an exposed position and didn't pause to think it through.

'It's me, Marion!' she yelled as she knocked on the Control Centre door. 'Don't shoot!'

When she stepped back inside, Felix was sprawled in the lobby. His brother Jurgen had cut a length from a thick fire hose to make a tourniquet for his bloody leg. Sam had emerged from cover, and Diogo heard Marion's shout too.

'How did Robin get here?' Diogo asked, seeing three guards with arrows sticking out of them as Mike fired another warning barrage to keep the cops downhill at bay.

'It was me!' Marion spat. 'They're probably conscious, so make yourself useful and disarm them.'

Cut-Throat fumed as he backed out of the control room. 'Marion, this isn't the time to wander off to the toilet,' he roared.

Convinced she was surrounded by idiots, Marion ignored her dad and took charge as she leaned into the control room and looked at Jeanne.

'How long now?' Marion asked.

'Finish!' Jeanne answered, as she flicked lever to close the gates at Youlgreave. 'I couldn't get hold of Will Scarlock at the mall for some reason, so I contacted Lyla directly. Her team are in place. They'll climb the pylon and disconnect the castle's electricity supply a couple of minutes before the surge arrives.'

Marion looked at her dad. 'There's eight of us and one truck is shot to hell. Get the controller's car keys.'

'There's a riot van and carloads of cops down there,' Sam shouted from the entrance. 'Even with that big gun, we'll have a time shooting our way out.'

'This road is not a dead end,' Jeanne said. 'It passes the dam and leads to another exit used by workers down in the hydroelectric plant.'

'Could be more cops that way, for all we know,' Sam suggested, as Cut-Throat extracted the controller's car keys. 'Or stinger strips across the road.'

'The chopper landed,' Marion warned. 'If both exits are blocked, the only thing we can do is split up and try to get out of here on foot.'

'Forty kilometres,' Cut-Throat said. 'Great . . .'

Sam gave cover as Jurgen and Diogo lifted a groaning Felix into the back of the pickup, laying him out between the legs of the big gun. Cut-Throat walked to the staff parking at the side of the building and swore when he saw that the controller drove a battered electric micro-car.

Cut-Throat opened its tinny little door and peered inside. 'I won't fit behind the wheel,' he said.

'Nice wheels!' Diogo teased as he got in the big pickup. 'Brum, brum!'

'I'll drive,' Jeanne said.

Marion squeezed in the back, while Cut-Throat set the front passenger seat back as far as it would go and still wound up with his knees touching his beard. 'It's not a car, it's a washing machine,' he protested as its tiny motor whirred to life.

'Off we go!' Jeanne said. 'I had a car like this when I was at university in Paris. Cheap to run and no *taxe de pollution*!'

'Gimme a big V8 and stuff the rainforest,' Cut-Throat growled, as he yanked the assault rifle wedged painfully between his leg and the door and passed it to Marion in the back.

Mike gave another blast with the big gun to deter the cops as the pickup set off, passing the truck with the blown radiator and almost running over the female guard who'd been on the wrong end of Marion's bow.

'You're the only one with a bow and arrow,' Cut-Throat said, looking baffled.

Marion groaned, then shouted, 'I didn't go to the bathroom, Daddy. I snuck out and shot the guards while you were yelling at Sam.'

Marion watched her dad's expression in the driver's mirror as it changed from baffled to impressed until he finally said, 'Good girl!'

The road down towards the dam was steep and wet. The little electric car struggled to keep pace with Diogo's pickup, and skinny tyres and no lighting made the ride scary.

As they rounded a sharp bend, Marion saw a man and woman running uphill towards the Control Centre. Her first impression was that the man held a bazooka and was about to blow them to hell, but after a second to process she realised the weapon was a shoulder-mounted video camera.

'TV news,' Jeanne said.

'It must have been the news chopper,' Marion said, relieved. 'Not the ones Little John saw leaving the castle.'

Jeanne slammed on the brakes. Marion's face whumped against the back of the driver's headrest and the little car almost ploughed into the back of the pickup.

'My dodgy knee!' Cut-Throat groaned. 'Do you have to drive like a maniac?'

Diogo's truck had stopped at the end of the road. There were two rows of parked cars, a small building housing lifts down to the hydroelectric power plant in the dam's base, and a gate. The gate was identical to the one they'd entered at the other end of the road but, with Felix's lock-picking skills out of action, escape was down to Mike and his machine gun.

'What is that nut doing?' Marion yelled, covering her ears as the muscly little biker opened fire.

After blasting the gates open, Mike shredded the unmanned security post alongside, pumped several parked cars with bullets and vaporised a squirrel who had the misfortune of being in the wrong place at the wrong time.

'Just hope the cops don't come chasing,' Cut-Throat growled as they followed the pickup through smoke and carnage. 'A three-legged tortoise could outrun this crate.'

# 45. DIVERSION TACTICS

Azeem's first line of defence was a muddy embankment, originally built as a levee protecting mall parking lots from the river. The only way there without getting wet was a two-hundred-metre walk along a wall dividing two sections of car park.

A single concrete block wide, it had water lapping over the top. It would only take one misplaced boot to plunge into the water and since thirty Castle Guards had just landed, Robin couldn't hang around.

He ran until he caught up with a couple of other guys who'd heard Azeem's call for reinforcements. With no room to overtake, Matt caught up too.

'Left,' Azeem whispered when the men reached the embankment. 'Noise down. Don't shoot, shout or fart until I give the order.'

As Robin leaped over a patch of deep mud onto the embankment, another security officer treated the two men to dabs of face camouflage.

'I've got five explosive arrows left,' Robin whispered to Azeem. 'I can blow a chopper if I'm close enough.'

But Azeem had seen Matt, and looked furious. 'Why have you brought him?'

'Brat brought himself.' Robin sighed.

Azeem glowered at Matt. 'Your mum will *murder* me if you get hurt.'

'I'm as tall as Robin,' Matt said noisily, then jumped as about five camouflage-painted men shushed him.

'Go right,' Azeem told Robin. 'Climb a tree if you think it'll give you a better shot. But don't go into the water.'

'Booby traps.' Robin nodded, as a hand reached out and smeared his cheeks with camouflage paint.

'Rub it in good,' the woman in charge of camouflage said. 'Especially your forehead. It really catches the moonlight.'

Matt looked pleased with his dab of camouflage. Robin hoped Azeem would send Matt back, but she had a hundred things to deal with, and he figured that ordering the ten-year-old back across the wall was risky with Castle Guards closing in.

'I won't even have to get you back for this,' Robin hissed at Matt as they crept along the embankment past armed men and women lying on their bellies. 'When Marion hears, you're toast.'

This threat of Marion seemed to concern Matt more than disobeying Emma or scaring his mums had done. But he only had seconds to consider before there was a metallic clank out in the river, followed by an agonised scream.

The Castle Guards had been wading stealthily from their drop point, but as Robin and Matt dived face down in the mud, there was hysterical splashing and shouting. Then another clank and a scream.

'Bear traps!' a Castle Guard shouted from about thirty metres away.

'Taste of their own medicine,' a woman in the mud close to Robin whispered.

'Now!' Azeem shouted.

Three huge floodlights erupted from treetops, illuminating Castle Guards wading through thigh-deep water. The view from the embankment was obscured by vegetation, but there were observation platforms in the biggest trees and Azeem's best snipers only had to crack a couple of shots to send Castle Guards who hadn't been shot or bear-trapped into retreat.

The rapid victory seemed a huge anticlimax. Less than a dozen shots had been fired at Azeem's security team. None were accurate because of the blinding light in the Castle Guards' faces.

'Shoot over their heads,' Azeem ordered as the enemy retreated into deeper water. 'Do not give Sheriff Marjorie a chance to call us killers.'

Robin looked up and tutted at Matt's mischievous mud-caked grin.

'It's easy when you know the bad guys are coming,' Azeem said proudly, as she gave Robin a slap on the back. 'Be sure to thank your brother for the tip-off.'

But joy turned to surprise as the splash of retreating Castle Guards was overpowered by the second chopper coming out of the dark and dropping towards the mall roof. A sliding door on the side of the chopper was wide open. As it skimmed the mall roof, three Castle Guards flung out metal drums, like mini beer kegs, that caught the moonlight.

'What are those?' Matt asked.

After ten seconds for the flammable liquid inside each cylinder to spread over the mall roof, a spark ignitor set it ablaze.

Teams on the roof took potshots at the helicopter, but had no weapons big enough to damage it. Robin could have shot explosive arrows, or hit and deflected some of the falling drums, but he was now too far away.

As twenty volcano-like fires erupted across one side of the Designer Outlets' roof, the helicopter turned to finish the job by dropping drums along the other side of the H.

# 46. LOBSTER AND CHIPS

Little John opened the penthouse door to a tweed-suited guard and a room service trolley laden with a jumbo buttered lobster roll, fries, Rage Cola and melting citrus pudding with ice cream.

'I'll wheel it inside,' John told the waiter, then tilted the basket of fries towards his guard. 'Chip?' he offered defiantly.

'No, thank you, Mr Kovacevic,' the guard answered politely, then added, 'I had a call to say that your mother has changed her plans. Her helicopter will arrive shortly.'

As the apartment door slammed behind him, John wheeled the trolley into his room and wondered if he'd ever eat lavish Sherwood Castle room service again. He'd packed a bag on the assumption that he might have to leave in a hurry, and his TV was tuned to Channel Fourteen News.

Correspondent Lynn Hoapili stood with Darley Dale Dam in the background and gusts of hilltop wind making a mess of her hair. A yellow and black 'BREAKING NEWS' banner flashed at the bottom of the screen.

'This is what we know so far,' Lynn said excitedly, as John slumped on his bed. 'About an hour ago, a large gang stormed the building to my right, which is the main Control Centre for the four historic dams in the Macondo Basin.

'The gang's intentions are not clear at this time, but we believe they gained control of computers inside, opening flood gates to release billions of litres of water. Police and dam security officers were on the scene quickly. Three were shot and seriously wounded by a young boy whose description closely matches that of Robin Hood . . .'

'Nice one, Robin,' John said, toasting his brother with his frosty glass of cola, while crumbs from the lobster roll spilled down his shirt.

As John dunked fries in Thousand Island dressing, the lights and the TV went off. After two seconds the lights came back on, along with a siren in the lift elevator lobby.

As John dashed across the room to look out of his window, a flash shot up from ground level, followed by a thud that made the windows shake.

*Looks like I pulled it off . . .*

There were whirrs and bursts of static as everything powered down, except the battery-powered emergency light above his door.

A pre-recorded announcement came from the elevator lobby as John reached for a torch, which he'd kept close by since sabotaging the generator.

'Sherwood Castle Resort wishes to apologise for this temporary power outage. Please remain where you are and await further announcements.'

John's bedroom felt eerie in the dark. He heard his mum's helicopter approach as he took the metal keep-warm lid off his pudding. He'd polished it off by the time the apartment's main door clicked and Moshe stepped into the emergency-lit hallway, a step ahead of his mother.

'Phase one was to wipe out the control tower,' Moshe told Marjorie confidentially. 'That idiot Scarlock ran his show from a tent in the middle of the roof! Then we landed a chopper with a bunch of guards out front. That was to draw mall security out of position before the second chopper dropped nitro-glycerine cylinders along the rooftop. By the time they flew out, Designer Outlets looked like a barbecue pit!'

'None of this can be tracked back to us?' Marjorie asked.

'It's all deniable,' Moshe said. 'Unknown group chartered the helicopters. We'll say we believe it's a violent territorial dispute between groups of forest bandits. Our heroic Castle Guards tried to intervene but came under heavy fire and four were injured in the rebels' savage bear traps . . .'

'Nicely spun,' Marjorie said, then squinted as a torch beam lit her face. Her gaze tracked the beam to Little John in his bedroom doorway.

'Not in my eyes,' Marjorie said irritably.

John angled the beam towards Moshe. 'What's up with the electric?'

'Power outage,' Moshe said. 'Back-up generator glitched. Someone from maintenance will whack it with a spanner and get it going.'

John was concerned by the news that Designer Outlets had been torched, though Channel Fourteen placed Robin forty kilometres away at Darley Dale Dam.

Another announcement came out of the lift lobby, this time from a real person. 'Sherwood Castle Resort again wishes to apologise for the power outage. Our dedicated team will restore current as quickly as possible. In the meantime, please avoid moving around the building, as the emergency lighting is limited and it may be difficult to see where you are going.'

As the announcement ended, John wondered if he was imagining a rumbling sound. But Marjorie glanced down, like she'd heard it too.

'The floor is shaking,' Marjorie said, sounding curious. She headed briskly for the balcony doors at the far end of the hallway. 'Moshe?'

'Wind,' Moshe suggested with a shrug. 'You can't hear it when the ventilation is running.'

'Not like any wind I've ever heard!' Marjorie barked as she stepped out onto her balcony and heard rushing water.

John bit his lip, stifling a grin as he jogged after Moshe onto the puddled balcony, where they ate breakfast when it was sunny. The rushing sound grew louder, though it was hard to tell its direction because the forest canopy muffled the noise.

John got a better view over the side of the balcony. This vista included the eighteenth hole of the resort's fanciest golf course and its mock-Tudor clubhouse.

The first water spilling along the manicured driveway caught the moonlight and looked glassy, but moments later a churning muddy wash almost a metre deep burst from the trees.

'How?' Marjorie shouted to Moshe, shaking with rage.

John leaned further over the balcony, catching the best view as water swallowed the clubhouse patio, washing away outdoor furniture and ripping sliding glass doors from their frames before engulfing the fancy lounge inside.

'Get my guards out of the basement levels,' Moshe shouted into his radio.

Marjorie glowered at Moshe. 'You said Hood was targeting the pumps yesterday. Please tell me they're working.'

Moshe looked uncharacteristically shaky as he gripped the balcony railing. 'I put guards on the pump room door and disabled remote access, but the pumps need electricity to work.'

Marjorie looked like she was about to explode. 'Could the rebels cut a power line and sabotage the back-up generator instead?'

'I suppose . . . I suppose that's possible.'

As John enjoyed Moshe's anguish, the water spewing across the golf course was now over a metre deep and had reached a guest parking lot, lifting cars and smashing them into the building.

'Imbecile!' Marjorie screamed at Moshe. 'You burn a worthless shuttered mall while the rebels destroy a two-billion-pound resort business!'

'Once the pumps are back online, they can probably empty the basements,' Moshe said.

'After how much damage?' Marjorie growled. 'I almost fired you when the rebels dropped smoke bombs into my trophy hunt. This is the last straw. You're done!'

The water kept rushing as Moshe shook his head. 'I worked fifty, sixty hours a week for you,' he spat. 'I've blackmailed, cajoled, bribed and built you a private army. If I showed the world the dirt I have on you, you won't be president – you'll be in the women's cell block on Pelican Island.'

John gawped as Marjorie's huge palm slapped Moshe's cheek. 'You've been well paid for everything you've done,' Marjorie roared over a background track of screams, smashing glass and car alarms. 'If I go down, you'll be two steps behind.'

'If I'm going to jail, it might as well be for murder,' Moshe said, reaching for the gun holstered inside his jacket.

Marjorie was fast like her son, snatching a glass candle holder off the breakfast table and using it to smash Moshe in the chin. But the former special forces officer was built tough, taking the blow and holding his gun centimetres from Marjorie's nose.

# 47. HAPPY HYPOXIA

As fires intensified and merged, Designer Outlets' fibreglass roof released the oil from its plastic base as choking black smoke. The mall was part-flooded inside and much of the way around, but this water was no use for firefighting without hoses and pumps to bring it up to the roof.

Unai knew the battle was lost, and ordered a full evacuation before the helicopter was out of earshot.

As the firefighters and defenders ran from ladders or slid from ropes, sprinkler heads melted and began misting the hallways inside. This moisture cooled the air and tamped the smoke for a couple of crucial minutes while the mall's long-term residents and the few remaining refugees evacuated without serious injury.

Once the frail, injured and patients in the clinic had been carried or wheeled to the northern parking lots, some went back into the thickening smoke for their belongings.

'The whole roof could collapse,' Unai warned, the skin on his arms and forehead toasted red from battling flames. 'Nothing in there is worth your life.'

Robin, Matt, Azeem and the others on the embankment waded and swam, or ran across the wall, to help out.

As Robin leaped off the wall, some security officers were risking running through the smoke-filled atrium to reach their families, but the intense heat scared Robin and he stuck with the majority, trudging through the mud and shallow water around the mall's edge.

After a breathless walk with smoke burning his eyes, Robin and Matt reached the unflooded northern parking lots. Most people had moved to the far end to escape the vile smoke. But a group of five stood just behind the mall. Robin was intrigued, because dozens of the chickens he looked after ran around nearby.

'What's this?' Robin asked nobody in particular.

Everyone backed up as a chunk of the roof at the north end of the mall caved and unleashed an intense jet of trapped smoke and water vapour. At the same moment, three well-fed birds flew off the rooftop, fluttering their wings gracelessly but landing unharmed.

Chicken Sheila stood in the broad gutter at the roof's edge, her face bright red and her crazy white hair now crazy blackened hair.

'Use the fire escape!' people were shouting.

'Sheila,' Robin shouted furiously when he saw. 'Get down, now!'

Although many were shouting, Robin caught Sheila's attention.

'You're supposed to be my assistant,' Sheila shouted furiously. 'Get up here and help me.'

Matt tutted. 'She's finally gone off her hinges.'

Robin glanced down the side of the mall and saw the metal fire-escape steps people were pointing at.

'Sheila, you're always complaining that everyone thinks you're crazy,' Robin yelled up. 'If you don't come down, you *are* crazy.'

'They're all huddled together in shock,' Sheila yelled back. 'My babies are burning.'

'Don't!' Robin shouted desperately as Sheila went back into the smoke.

'Robin, you can't help,' someone shouted as he ran towards the fire stairs.

Heat from inside the mall made the metal handrail hot to touch. They only went up as far as a fire exit on the mall's upper floor, so when Robin got to the top he balanced on the handrail and reached for the gutter at the roof's edge. But his height let him down. He was surprised when Matt grabbed his boot.

'Step on my shoulder,' Matt said, his voice gruff from the smoke.

'Don't you dare!' Indio yelled at Robin as she ran towards the bottom of the steps. 'And, Matthew Maid, you are in *big* trouble.'

Robin ignored Indio, letting Matt push him up, then walking along the broad gutter at the roof's edge, while the wind mercifully whipped most smoke away from him. The roof felt solid, but the heat trapped beneath created currents of hot air, like a hairdryer blasting his soggy tracksuit legs.

'Matt, Robin!' Indio yelled again, as a growing crowd of adults urged them to get down too. 'Don't be so bloody stupid.'

Robin saw Sheila come out of the smoke holding another pair of chickens.

'About time you pulled your finger out,' Sheila said, smiling madly as she leaned over the edge of the roof to give her precious flapping birds the shortest possible flight to safety. 'See how many you can spot with those young eyes of yours.'

'You have to come down,' Robin said strongly, as Matt crept up behind him. 'This roof could cave at any second.'

'They are my babies,' Sheila repeated.

The skin on Sheila's face was blistered, but she seemed weirdly happy. Matt remembered a documentary about finding an old shipwreck. In the film, one of the divers didn't get enough oxygen and kept laughing and giggling.

'It's happy hypoxia,' Matt told Robin.

'What?'

'When you don't get enough air, you go nuts,' Matt explained. 'She's as high as a kite.'

As Sheila stumbled back towards the smoke, Robin grabbed her under the arms. His boot made a ripping sound and he realised that just standing still for two seconds had made it melt into the roof.

'No!' Sheila squealed.

Robin feared that Sheila would knock him one way to the ground, or the other onto the melting roof, but the feisty old woman was bony and weak.

'You big bullies!' Sheila screamed as Matt picked up her legs and the pair carried her back towards the stairs.

'We'll find the best chicken sheds in Sherwood Forest,' Robin said, stifling a cough as he walked crabwise. 'I'll help you every day, OK?'

'Don't patronise me, you little turd!' Sheila screamed. 'Let go of me.'

Robin worried they'd have to drop Sheila down onto the hot metal steps, but burly ex-Locksley police officer Mr Khan had climbed the steps and gripped Sheila's legs before lowering her gently over his shoulder.

'I'll sue the lot of you!' Sheila shouted, swatting Mr Khan on the back as he ran down the steps. 'I'll drag you through the highest courts in the land.'

Robin and Matt jumped easily from the gutter to the stairs. But when Robin clanked down, his boot had zero grip and he skidded into the hot handrail. When Matt gave him a hand up, Robin saw that the bottom of his boots were coated in the melted grey surface of the roof.

Mr Khan put Sheila on the ground and several people gathered to calm her down as Robin and Matt confronted Indio's furious eyes and wagging finger.

'Don't you ever . . .' she roared, then burst into tears as she pulled the two smoky, sweaty, camouflage-painted boys into her chest for a desperate hug.

'I was worried about you two,' Indio sobbed. 'We carried Zack and Finn out, then helped Liz get her little ones down the escalator. There was no time to get any of our stuff.'

Otto arrived and looked disappointed. 'Why are you hugging Matt? You said you were gonna to kill him!'

'Promise you'll never do that again,' Indio said, as she gripped Robin's shoulder.

Robin had lost another home, his boots were smoking and everything was gone apart from his bow, phone and whatever random junk was in his backpack, but he saw the funny side.

'I promise,' Robin said, smiling. 'The next time a building is on fire and a crazy lady is throwing chickens off the roof, I won't get involved.'

But Matt seemed more serious. 'What the hell do we do now?'

Robin looked around and saw what Marion's skinny little brother meant. Designer Outlets was done for and they were deep in the forest, in a parking lot covered with litter, ashes and broken tents left by fleeing refugees.

'Let's get away from this smoke, at least,' Indio said.

'You're a true hero,' a tearful woman told Robin, as she tousled his hair and handed him a bottle of drinking water.

The river was toxic and their drinking water had been destroyed, so the gift was a generous one. Robin could have happily guzzled the lot, but he drank half, splashed his stinging eyes and zipped the rest in his pack for later as they reached the crowded area furthest from the smoke.

Karma gave Robin a hug when they reached the rest of the Maid family. He sat on the remains of an abandoned tent that they were using as a ground sheet and used his pocketknife to dig chunks of melted roof from the treads of his boots.

He checked his phone, but Wi-Fi and phone signals had bitten the dust when the masts and dishes on the watchtower fell.

Twenty metres in one direction, a makeshift medical centre used limited supplies to deal with smoke inhalation and people who'd been injured when the atrium roof collapsed. Twenty metres the other, Will, Emma, Azeem and other senior figures in the Designer Outlets community circled up for a lively meeting.

Robin thought about helping the injured, but he was exhausted. He used his backpack for a pillow and Finn snuggled up to him as Will made a sharp double clap.

'May I have everyone's attention?' Will began. Robin noticed tear streaks down the leader's sooty face. 'Our homes and fifteen years of my life are ablaze, but I've got an idea.'

# 48. THE DEVIL YOU KNOW

Moshe pulling the gun opened every adrenaline gland in Little John's body.

*If Moshe shoots Mum, he'll shoot me next to cover his tracks.*

*If I run he'll shoot me in the back.*

*My chances aren't great, but if I don't act now, I'm 100% dead . . .*

The marble-topped breakfast table was too heavy to flip, but the padded outdoor dining chairs had some heft. John grabbed one with a beefy arm and flung it towards Moshe with everything he had.

Moshe fired a shot as the chair flew over the table and hit him hard. Marjorie stumbled backwards. John hurled another chair then came at Moshe low, like he was making a rugby tackle.

As he thumped Moshe against the balcony railings, John expected to see his mum wounded or dead, but she was on her feet as he tried to keep Moshe pinned.

Unfortunately, the Israeli former soldier had moves and smashed a wicked elbow into the side of John's head.

John was dazed, but as Moshe tried to move his dead weight, Marjorie snatched a lump of broken chair and used it to knock Moshe's head against the railings. Then she grabbed Moshe by his belt and collar and lifted him until his torso hung out over the balcony.

'No!' Moshe gasped, he tried to grab hold of the balcony rail.

As John picked the gun off the wooden decking, Marjorie lifted Moshe's legs over the railing, leaving him dangling by one hand. As he looked up pleadingly, Marjorie didn't miss a beat and stomped his grasping fingers.

'Man!' John gasped, stumbling to the railings as Moshe's body clattered into the treetops.

'Nice teamwork,' Marjorie said, smiling a little as she placed a hand on her heart and drew a slow breath.

'You've got moves,' John said admiringly. 'I was sure he'd shot you.'

'Grew up in three care homes and a dozen foster families,' Marjorie said. 'You learn to scrap, because there's always someone stealing your headphones or trying to cop a feel.'

John's loyalties were more scrambled than ever. He'd ruined his mum's plans by sabotaging the generator, then saved her from a bullet.

As Marjorie and John caught their breath, Jeanne's computer-modelled four-and-a-half-minute surge slowed to a muddy trickle.

'Did you decide whose side you're on?' Marjorie asked John coldly.

John didn't answer the question.

'I saved your life,' he noted.

Marjorie seemed satisfied. 'I need to act fast, and your help would be appreciated.'

'What do you want?'

'Sherwood Castle Resort is done. Guests will never come back after this. King Corporation will pull the plug and kick me off the board of directors.'

'What about your plan to turn the resort into a prison?' John asked.

'It's probably not viable with three levels of flooded basement to repair. And if I'm going to launch a presidential campaign without King Corporation's support, I need money in weeks, not years.'

John sensed his mother's confidence. 'You have a plan?'

'Always have a plan,' Marjorie advised her son. 'And a back-up plan for when things go wrong. Right now I need strong arms to carry things down to the helicopter pad.'

'Carry what?' John asked.

'Art,' Marjorie said, stepping back into the hallway. 'There are eleven paintings here, worth approximately one hundred and thirty million pounds. The Jackson

Pollock is too big to fit in the helicopter, but we can take the others.

'I know an art dealer in Qatar who can sell them quickly and discreetly. By the time King Corporation realises that their paintings are gone from the castle . . .'

John gawped as he followed his mum inside. 'I thought these paintings were yours.'

Marjorie laughed. 'Another piece of advice, son. Never buy things with your own money when you can use someone else's. The paintings were purchased using a complicated ownership structure that King Corporation uses to avoid tax. If Richard King decides to sue me to get his paintings back, it will take years and his sneaky tax dodges will be out in the open.'

'So basically, you're stealing a hundred million quid from King Corporation and there's not much they can do?'

'In a nutshell,' Marjorie agreed. 'Get the paintings down, and pack yourself a bag with anything important. We won't be coming back here.'

As John lifted a Joan Miró pastel drawing off the wall, Marjorie opened the apartment door and gave orders to the guard outside. 'Go down to the helipad and tell my pilots to be ready in ten minutes. Then come straight back here. I need you to help us carry things down to the pad.'

'Yes, Madam Sheriff,' the guard said, before rushing off.

'It'll be Madam President before we know it,' Marjorie joked to her son, as she came back inside and found that

John had already stacked the five smallest paintings by the door.

'We'll stay at the Sheriff's residence in Nottingham tonight. You can order yourself a fancy new phone and laptop before King Corporation cancels my expenses account.'

It was closer to twenty minutes by the time the artworks were loaded in the helicopter. Marjorie had stuffed a large trunk with personal belongings, and the guard returned from a trip to retrieve the contents of a safe in Moshe's apartment three floors down.

'You never left this door,' Marjorie told the guard as she wheeled her case out of the apartment. 'You did nothing, you saw nothing.'

Then she dropped a diamond necklace into his palm. 'The setting is nothing special but the stones are a good size. Aitkenhead & Sons in Nottingham will pay a decent price for them.'

'Thank you, madam,' the guard said, and looked chuffed as he dropped the necklace into his blazer pocket.

Marjorie looked back into the apartment. 'John, why am I waiting?' she yelled.

John was in his room, feeling anxious as he stuffed schoolbooks and some of his favourite clothes into an extra bag. He felt like he'd forgotten something, and at the last second doubled back and picked a framed picture of Robin, his dad and Auntie Pauline from the bedside table.

The lifts and power were still out, so it was six flights of gloomy stairs down to the helipad.

'I'm afraid our flight to Nottingham will take extra time,' the co-pilot announced, as John ducked into the wood and leather luxury of King Corporation's eight-seat VIP helicopter. 'There's a huge fire at the old outlet mall and we'll have to fly around the smoke.'

'Safety first,' Marjorie agreed, as she threw her wheeled suitcase aboard and checked that the stacked paintings were well secured.

John clicked his seatbelt as they lifted off. He'd flown out of the Castle after dark many times, but it looked ghostly with no lights and muddy pools over the hunting grounds and golf courses.

As they blasted away, John saw the flashing lights of three approaching fire engines and hundreds of evacuated staff milling outside the lobby, from waiters and kitchen hands to the Castle Guards, whose basement quarters were now under several metres of water.

'We had fun while it lasted,' Marjorie joked, taking a pack of cashews from a snack tray as Sherwood Castle shrank into the distance.

# 49. FOR THE PEOPLE

By ten the next morning, the flood and evacuation of Sherwood Castle was old news. Partly because Jeanne's careful planning had resulted in zero serious injuries at the castle or upriver, and partly because, after months of record-breaking rain, the public weren't interested in stories about floods.

Channel Fourteen reporter Lynn Hoapili had been working since five the previous evening and felt exhausted as she helped her camera operator Oluchi take down light stands and wind cables in front of Sherwood Castle. Two of the three national news organisations had already left, and the third only remained because their van had broken down and they were waiting for a recovery truck.

In the background were three fire trucks. Fire officers wandered around, stepping over pipes pumping brown water from the castle lobby. Lynn felt her phone vibrate and saw a message from a news wire.

'King Corporation announce closure of Sherwood Castle Resort,' Lynn read aloud to her disinterested camera operator. 'Seven hundred and thirty full- and part-time staff received the news early this morning via text message. King Corp press officer Miles Ngoy said that reopening the resort was unlikely due to difficult trading conditions and continued operational issues.'

'Anything about Sheriff Marjorie getting kicked off their board?' Oluchi asked.

'Not yet,' Lynn said, cracking a big yawn as she reached into the back of the broadcast van and put rolled-up cables on hooks. 'God, I need coffee.'

Oluchi, who still looked perky, smiled.

'You'll understand when you're ancient like me,' Lynn said.

'Pity there was no CCTV of Robin Hood shooting cops at Darley Dale Dam,' Oluchi said. '*That* would have made it a big story!'

Lynn smiled and nodded. 'Everyone loves a Robin Hood story.'

Fifty metres across the resort driveway, Lynn noticed the team from National Broadcast Network getting excited. She guessed it was their recovery truck until she spotted a convoy of vehicles driving fast on the broad and immaculately tarmacked road that led between Route 24 and the castle.

'Oluchi, get your camera back out,' Lynn spat eagerly, as she realised the convoy had over twenty vehicles, led by a pair of Brigand bikes and a black pickup with a 50mm machine gun mounted in the back.

'I've got one battery on twenty-six per cent and one on nineteen,' Oluchi moaned from inside the van. 'I thought you wanted coffee.'

'This is not a drill,' Lynn yelled, as she stood on the van's rear platform to get a higher viewpoint. She counted a dozen bashed-up trucks, six luxury cars, several tattier cars, loads of bikes and a trio of Locksley city buses at the rear.

'Interesting!' Oluchi noted when she saw what Lynn was seeing, and dived around the front to get her camera.

Lynn frantically dialled her studio on her mobile. 'I've got something,' she yelled. 'Can you get me on live?'

As the convoy drew nearer, Oluchi realised she'd get the best shot of the convoy by standing on top of the van.

'I see a very big gun,' Oluchi said warily. 'But nobody behind it.'

Tired fire crews stared as Brigand bikes with no mufflers blasted by and stopped in front of Sherwood Castle Resort. Oluchi slid down off the van roof and Lynn jostled for the best spot with the NBN reporter as bodies started getting out of the convoy vehicles, most with filthy clothes and smoke-darkened faces.

'Who are they?' Oluchi asked.

'No idea,' Lynn said. 'Keep filming.'

The NBN crew spotted Robin Hood get out of a large Mercedes, with Marion right behind him. He was in a state, stained with mud, soot and everything between.

'Robin Hood,' the NBN reporter said enthusiastically. 'You are live on NBN News. How do you feel about the three people you shot and wounded last night at Darley Dale Dam?'

'Wasn't me,' Robin said, as he gave Oluchi's camera a thumbs-up. 'Good to see you, Lynn! Go, Channel Fourteen!'

'I shot them,' Marion hissed in Robin's ear. 'You get the credit for everything!'

Robin laughed and whispered back, 'I can't help being amazing.'

Will Scarlock emerged from a six-door limousine that still had a Guy Gisborne Luxury Autos price sticker in the side window. The camera operators realised that Will was going to make an announcement, as several dozen bikers and Forest People lined up behind him.

More refugees and former mall residents poured out of the buses as Will began to speak to the news cameras.

'In recent months, people like me who call Sherwood Forest home have faced record-breaking rainfall. This situation has been made worse by the Macondo Water Authority releasing floodwater in a deliberately reckless manner, leading to erosion, mudslides and unnecessary flooding.

'Thousands of Forest People have been forced to leave our homes. Last night Sherwood Designer Outlets, which has long been a hub providing essential services like healthcare and educational resources, was burned to the ground by thugs working for Sheriff Marjorie.

'As we made our way here this morning, we heard that Sherwood Castle is no longer of use to the billionaire brothers who own King Corporation. Well, let me tell you, the facilities here at Sherwood Castle are useful if you have no roof over your head. If you have no food or fresh water. If you have no school or healthcare for your children. Or if you are an orphan child whose parents were killed in a mudslide.

'So I, Will Scarlock, hereby claim Sherwood Castle as the property of the people of Sherwood Forest!'

'And God help anyone who tries to take it back!' Cut-Throat added from behind.

Cheers erupted, Brigands fired shots in the air, and several people scooped Will off the ground. The TV crews followed as Will was carried up the steps and lowered onto the soggy carpet in the castle's hotel-style lobby.

'We'll soon get the power restored and the water pumped from the basements,' Will said resolutely.

Robin ducked around the outside of the crowd as far from the TV cameras as he could get, then began to sprint towards a staircase.

'What are you up to?' Marion asked suspiciously as she chased after him.

'Eighth floor,' Robin said, smirking. 'I bagsy the penthouse, and if you're *extremely* lucky I might let you share it.'

273

# 50. THE SHERIFF'S SPIN

Two weeks after Will Scarlock seized Sherwood Castle for the people of Sherwood Forest, six thousand of Sheriff Marjorie's most fanatical supporters stood in a Nottingham concert arena, waving metallic balloons, handmade placards and giant foam hands.

'Ladies aaaaaaand gentlemen,' an announcer in a garish velvet jacket screamed from a giant stage with stacks of flashing lights. 'I am incredibly honoured to introduce you to our country's next president, Sheriff Marjorie Kovacevic!'

Marjorie walked on stage to screams, shouts and phone flashes. She wore a business-like trouser suit, red heels carefully matched to her lipstick, and a new hairdo with highlights.

'Thank you, thank you!' Marjorie said, dabbing at a fake tear as the blast of applause continued. 'You people are my light in these dark times.'

She paused dramatically until the crowd went silent and the arena lights were dimmed in anticipation of her next words.

'Because these *are* dark times,' Marjorie boomed dramatically. 'We have been crippled by unemployment, inflation, taxation and immigration! Less than twenty kilometres from here, we have lost control of our own country. A quarter of a million terrorists, immigrants and dirtbags live as outlaws in Sherwood Forest. First they stole our jobs and destroyed the healthcare and schools that our taxes pay for.

'When we said *no way*, they took over Sherwood Castle, blew up the access roads and dared us to take it back. Well, let me tell you, when I am president there will be no standing for this nonsense. What will we say?'

'No way!' six thousand shouted back.

'I can't hear you,' Marjorie said, cupping one ear. 'What will we say?'

'No way!' the crowd blasted.

'I am back in Nottingham today to make a very special announcement. Sadly, the electoral commission says I must stand down as Sheriff when I run for president.'

The crowd booed softly and made 'ahh' noises.

'But I am here to announce my endorsement for an incredibly talented replacement. A man I have known since I was a tiny eight-year-old girl, standing barely three metres tall.'

Comedians and the media often made jokes about Sheriff Marjorie's size, and the adoring crowd loved that she could laugh about it herself.

'This candidate is a man who has helped turn Locksley from one of the nation's most deprived areas into a dynamic city with an expanding world-class university and an incredible technological hub for ecologically sound waste disposal. Let us give a big cheer to our People's Party candidate for Sheriff of Nottingham, Mr Guy Gisborne!'

As the crowd cheered, Guy Gisborne stepped on stage in a smart black suit, clean-shaven with a tight new haircut. He was followed by his wife, two tween sons dressed in suits and his daughter Clare in a smart black and white dress and – after she refused to wear heels – a pair of black Converse sneakers.

'And since our next sheriff has his family on stage,' Marjorie said, 'let's hear it for my own son, the very dashing Mr John Kovacevic!'

As Guy Gisborne waved and smiled and tossed out hats printed with his *Let's Whip Sherwood into Shape* campaign slogan, Little John stepped on stage in a nicely cut suit, with a pained expression and his cheeks ablaze with embarrassment.

Clare flashed John an *I wish I was dead too* look as he lined up on stage next to her.

'What do we say?' Sheriff Marjorie and Guy Gisborne yelled in unison.

As the crowd shouted 'No way!', Clare held John's hand, a gesture hidden from the crowd by her little brother's torso.

Clare said something quietly.

'Can't hear over this noise,' John said, bending down to get closer to Clare's mouth. 'Sorry.'

Clare cupped a hand around her mouth and slowly repeated the words. 'I love you.'

She'd never said it before. John felt tears well in his eyes as he quietly mouthed, 'I love you too.'

Look out for

# ROBIN HOOD

**RANSOMS, RAIDS & REVENGE**

**Read on for an extract . . .**

# 5. WHAT WOULD ROBIN DO?

Matt Maid was a skinny ten-year-old who liked to talk big. But while achievements on a skateboard or playing Call of Duty might impress his mates, Matt now faced grown-up decisions.

It was pure luck that Matt had missed the bandits' ambush. Ten Man had asked him to start clearing up the equipment. A length of rope had slipped off Matt's shoulder when he jumped off the debris mound and he was on one knee coiling it back up when the four bandits jumped Ten Man.

As Matt crawled away, he saw two more bandits ambush Lyla and poke a rifle between her shoulder blades. When the powerful dog knocked Robin down, Matt felt sure someone would grab him from behind or aim a gun and order him to freeze. But one minute later Matt sat breathlessly on the snowy tiles with his back against the low concrete around the atrium's fountain.

As he brushed beads of shatterproof glass off his padded trousers, his first thought was to phone for help. But few spots in the forest had a signal, so it was no surprise when he peeked at the phone inside his jacket and saw a red X on the signal bar.

Matt's next idea was to run. He'd lived in the forest his whole life, and while he'd never been this far from home on his own, he was confident he'd be able to navigate back to Sherwood Castle. But it would take two hours, and then he'd have to explain what had happened and get back with a rescue team. By which time Robin, Lyla and Ten Man would be long gone.

*Can't abandon them*, Matt thought. *What would Robin do?*

Thinking about Robin dented Matt's confidence. It wasn't just that Robin was older, or a fearless climber, or a better shot with a bow and arrow. Robin had a special aura. Most kids froze when things got dangerous, but that's when Robin thrived.

*I'm not Robin.*

*I can't fix this.*

*I still climb in Mum's bed when I get nightmares.*

A deep male roar boomed in the distance. Matt peeked over the concrete wall and saw that Ten Man had tried to break loose as his four captors jumped off the debris mound. The mean dog started barking and the woman with the rifle – the one who'd captured Lyla – closed in and aimed at Ten Man's chest.

'I'll blow your head off!' she shouted. 'You ain't worth nothing.'

Seeing the woman point the gun made Matt consider his enemy. The bandits were filthy and raggedly dressed. He'd escaped, which meant their ambush was poorly planned. And why would you send four guys to wrestle Ten Man, when they could have just pointed a gun at him?

*Because they only have one gun . . . Two now they've taken Lyla's rifle . . .*

Matt felt a touch more confident as he watched eight bandits, three captives and a mean dog exit through the remains of the mall's main entrance, then head across the south parking lot towards a riverside camp and the smoking fire he'd spotted when they first arrived.

He was outnumbered and his only weapon was a little utility knife, but Matt felt sure he was facing lightly armed bandits who'd got lucky, rather than some elite crew dispatched to claim the bounty on Robin's head.

*I can do this*, Matt told himself as he stood up.

*I may not be Robin Hood, but I'm not stupid and I've got surprise on my side.*

*But what exactly do I do?*

After glancing around, Matt hopped over the fountain wall and made a crouching run back towards the debris mound. The bandit crew had grabbed the equipment around the hole, including Matt's own backpack and

Robin's bow, but they hadn't bothered with Ten Man's extra-large pack down at floor level.

It was too heavy for Matt to lift, so he dragged it to a less open spot and rummaged. There was no sign of the gun he'd hoped to find, but he took a bigger knife, a canteen of water, a small pair of binoculars and a lighter.

Pockets bulged and the binoculars swung around Matt's neck as he set off towards the bandit camp. After a flat-out sprint across the precariously exposed parking lot, he reached a long earth levee built to stop floodwater from reaching the mall.

Snow crunched as he lay at the top of the sloped embankment and raised the binoculars to his eyes. The bandit camp was a fragile affair, set way too close to the stream. Three shacks had been built from plastic sheeting and debris from the mall. There was fishing gear with lines in the icy water, a tatty open-hulled motorboat, a pair of red gas cylinders and the large smoking fire.

Around the fire was well-trodden ground, where snow and mud had been trampled to a slushy mess. Ten Man and Lyla had been ordered to sit cross-legged in this dirt, guarded by a jittery middle-aged man, who seemed to have rushed out of bed before putting his outdoor clothes on.

Matt eyed backpacks and gear on the ground near the fire, including his own pack and Robin's bow. In another sign of the bandits' lack of organisation, Ten Man seemed free to move his arms around, and while Matt's view of Lyla was obscured, he felt sure she wasn't tied up either.

While the adult captives were being ignored, Robin got all the attention. He was twenty metres from the fire, surrounded by excited bandits who made him kneel with hands behind his head. While older bandits huddled up, discussing their next step, three grubby lads in their late teens tormented Robin, posing for selfies and making threats.

Matt couldn't hear every word, but one lad had sliced a big clump of hair from the back of Robin's head and was making a joke about selling it online to the young hero's admirers.

'We'd make more if we cut off his ear,' another joked, before putting his boot against Robin's back and knocking him face first into the icy dirt.

'Don't break him, he's worth money,' an older woman shouted from the huddle.

'Dirtbags,' Matt muttered to himself, feeling more determined than scared as one lad yanked Robin up by the back of his hoodie and laughed at the muddy snow streaking down his face.

# 6. COOKING WITH GAS

With all but one bandit focused on Robin, Matt reckoned he should focus on helping Ten Man and Lyla. The ten-year-old knew he had no chance if he attacked head on, so figured his best shot was to distract their single nervous guard and give them a chance to break loose.

*But what if I'm wrong?*

*What if Robin gets killed?*

*What if . . . ?*

*Maybe I should run and get help.*

Matt gulped, then stood up and tried to imagine himself as a hero.

*I can be like Robin. He's not superhuman . . .*

Matt clambered over the top of the levee and kept low as he scrambled through trees and bushes towards the tents on the riverbank. Snow crunching and branches cracking under his boots seemed loud, but nobody heard as he reached riverbank mud with a delicate sheet of ice on top.

He'd seen no sign of life inside the tents through the binoculars, but Matt's nerves still jangled as he approached the shack at the far edge. It was the largest of the three and he squelched cautiously towards the back.

A rubber hose ran in from the red gas bottle outside the tent. Matt peered through the semi-translucent plastic sheeting to make sure nobody was inside, then made a slash with his knife and reached through.

The gas bottle was linked to a knee-height camping stove, with a heater at the front and two cooking rings on top. He pulled the rubber hose from the back of the stove and was pleased by a gentle hissing sound and a whiff of gas.

Cooking-gas fires were a hazard of forest life, and one of the strongest commandments of Matt's early childhood was to never-never-never touch or even go near a gas appliance. But he'd also witnessed a posse who'd been trying to capture Robin using a gas explosion as a very effective distraction . . .

As Matt waited nervously, wondering if the gas he could smell was poisonous and unsure how much needed to build up inside the tent to make a decent explosion, he could hear the bandits arguing about the best way to claim Robin's bounty.

In theory, Guy Gisborne had offered £250,000 to anyone who brought Robin Hood to him alive. But the gangster was notoriously untrustworthy and tight with money.

'Seriously think Gisborne's gonna pay a quarter million to you no-hopers?' Robin taunted. 'He'd sooner chop you up and feed you to his pigs.'

This earned Robin a crack around the head from one of the youths and a warning to shut his face.

Matt had backed away from the shack, but the gas smell was getting stronger and the bandits would surely smell it soon too. A thousand warnings from both of Matt's mothers ran through his brain as he pulled Ten Man's lighter from his pocket.

After squatting behind a rock and reading a reassuring sticker that said the lighter was *guaranteed wind resistant*, Matt couldn't help his hand trembling as he flung it towards the hole he'd cut in the plastic.

Before he could fully lower his head, a huge fireball shot up through surrounding trees and the shack's plastic skin vaporised. A screaming pregnant woman ran out of the furthest shack as its plastic roof turned to string cheese in the heat, but Matt had no time to pity her.

The backpacks were by the fire, less than ten metres from Matt's position. He squinted from heat and glare as he ran. As he'd hoped, Ten Man used the blast as an opportunity to wrap his arms around his guard and drive him head first into the frozen ground.

As Lyla grabbed a chunk of wood to use as a weapon and the bandits looked confused, Matt snatched up the pack with Robin's bow inside and kept running until he clattered into bushes. There was a shattering bang behind him as the overheated gas bottle ruptured, followed by crashing sounds as heat made chunks of rapidly melting snow fall down between tree branches.

Robin had taught him basic archery skills, and Matt was a decent shot from close range. His big worry was that one of the bandits would start shooting, but he couldn't spot either gun amidst the chaos so he took aim at the three lads who'd been tormenting Robin.

The torso is the easiest target and Matt hit the first teenager in the chest and the other in the shoulder as he turned away. The third guy fell as he tried to escape, but Matt's attempt to shoot him in the arse missed by a few centimetres.

'Don't shoot!' Robin shouted, hands aloft as he sprinted towards Matt.

Both boys ducked when they heard a gunshot, but when Matt looked around it was Lyla holding the gun. Ten Man took a bandit out with a single punch, then effortlessly picked two off the ground and knocked them out cold by bashing their heads together.

Robin had a muddy face and felt tearful as he looked at Matt, but he still managed a joke. 'Who said you could use my bow?'

Matt smiled back. 'Someone had to save your sorry arse.'

Lyla fired a warning shot into the air as the bandits scattered.

'Clear your stuff,' Ten Man shouted. 'Don't let me see any of you within fifty kilometres of here.'

'Not bad for Marion's annoying little brother,' Robin told Matt, giving him a big slap on the back. 'What blew up?'

'The old gas-bottle trick,' Matt explained.

Matt soaked up Robin's praise and cracked a huge smile. But reality kicked in as the youngster looked around the remains of the camp.

The scruffy little girl who'd surprised Robin on the debris mound was lost and screaming. The dog whimpered, the pregnant woman was having a panic attack and one of the sadistic teens bled from a huge chest wound with no chance of getting to a hospital.

Matt had done what was needed to rescue his friends, but the result didn't feel like something he should be proud of.

'Are we all healthy?' Ten Man asked, as he closed in on the boys with Lyla a few steps behind.

'I've had better mornings,' Lyla moaned, as Matt and Robin nodded wearily. 'Let's get our gear and march the hell out of here.'

Robert Muchamore's books have sold 15 million copies in over 30 countries, been translated into 24 languages and been number-one bestsellers in eight countries including the UK, France, Germany, Australia and New Zealand.

Find out more at
muchamore.com

Follow Robert
on Facebook and Twitter
@RobertMuchamore

**Discover more books and sign up to the Robert Muchamore mailing list at muchamore.com**

f muchamore

⊙ muchamorerobert

🐦 @robertmuchamore

Thank you for choosing a Hot Key book.

If you want to know more about our authors and what we publish, you can find us online.

You can start at our website

**www.hotkeybooks.com**

And you can also find us on:

**We hope to see you soon!**

# Robert Muchamore's
# ROBIN HOOD series

*More ROBIN HOOD adventures to come!*